Marsala

Magnolias

Mary Ellen and Antonio

The Hamiltons

Book Three

SJ McCoy

A Sweet n Steamy Romance

Published by Xenion, Inc

Published by Xenion, Inc.
First Paperback edition June 2018
www.sjmccoy.com

This book is a work of fiction. Names, characters, places, and events are figments of the author's imagination, fictitious, or are used fictitiously. Any resemblance to actual events, locales or persons living or dead is coincidental.

Cover Design by Dana Lamothe of Designs by Dana
Editor: Mitzi Pummer Carroll
Proofreaders: Aileen Blomberg and Marisa Nichols

ISBN 978-1-946220-38-7

Dedication

For MaryEllen and MaryEllen.

I know my Antonio could never hold a candle to yours, but I hope that he brings you both a smile.

With love

SJ

Chapter One

Mary Ellen opened the fridge and stared at its uninspiring contents. She'd been doing well, but the thought of yet another salad held no appeal. She opened the freezer and sighed. A neat pile of nutritious, low-calorie microwave dinners stared forlornly back at her. No. She couldn't force herself to do it. She closed the door firmly and smiled. "I'm going to Molly's," she announced to the empty apartment.

It had been a long week, and it was only Wednesday. Work was crazy because Cameron had a seemingly endless stream of candidates coming through the office every day. He was looking to appoint a new Sales Director and, as his right-hand woman, she'd been involved in every aspect of the process. Well, everything except the initial sorting of candidates. If she'd been part of that, David would have never made it past the paper sift. She gave herself a shake. Hadn't she just decided she was going to take herself out to Molly's for dinner? She picked up her purse and checked that she had her keys. She wasn't going to hang around here thinking about David. She'd done way too much of that when she first arrived in Napa. He was the past, and she could only hope that he wouldn't have any effect on her future. Surely Cameron would see through him when he sat down to interview him tomorrow.

She let herself out of the apartment and rode the elevator down to the lobby. Lately, she'd been making the effort to take the stairs, but tonight she was giving herself a night off. No salad, no stairs, nope. She was going to indulge herself in whatever she felt like tonight—everything except thinking about David.

She smiled when she stepped out onto the street. It was a warm, pleasant evening. She was lucky, and she knew it. She needed to focus on all the good in her life. She lived right here in Napa. She had an amazing job that she loved that allowed her to live in a fantastic apartment right downtown. There were people the world over who would give anything to live the life she was living. So what if her ex-fiancé was in town? So what if he was being considered for a job at Hamilton-Groves? She couldn't believe he'd get it, and even if by some strange twist of fate he did, he wouldn't have to affect her or the life she'd built for herself here.

She slid her keys into her purse and slung it over her shoulder as she set out toward Molly's. She wasn't going to allow him to spoil this evening for her. She was going to enjoy herself, eat something highly calorific, have a glass or two of something alcoholic and just relax. If it wasn't too busy, she might get to catch up with Molly and hear what was going on in her world.

Looking through the window when she arrived, she was surprised to see that Molly's was busy. Not crowded, but there were far more patrons than she'd expected to see this early on a Wednesday evening. Molly greeted her with a smile as she let herself in.

"Hey, girlfriend. Did some memo go out that Molly's is the place to be tonight?"

Mary Ellen laughed. "Maybe. If it did, it was some telepathic message, and I got it loud and clear."

"Well, you're not the only one." Molly looked around. "It's unusual to be this busy, but I'm not complaining. Where do you want to sit? Want to take the window and watch the world go by?"

Mary Ellen followed her toward a booth by the front window. "Is this okay?"

Mary Ellen shot a glance at the next booth which didn't have a window, but looked much quieter, tucked away in the corner.

She raised an eyebrow at her friend, but Molly made a face. "Sorry. It's taken. I think he must have gone to the bathroom, but he'll be back."

"Oh, no worries." Mary Ellen slid into the booth by the window. "This is great."

"What can I get you to drink?"

Mary Ellen grinned. "You know what I like when I'm by myself."

Molly chuckled and looked around. "Okay. Your secret's safe with me."

Once she'd gone, Mary Ellen studied the menu. She ate here often enough that she could probably recite the whole thing by heart, but after her recent attempts at dieting, just reading each of the delicious sounding dishes felt like a treat.

Molly returned after a few minutes and put a Margarita down in front of her. "There you go. It makes me laugh that you drink those when you come in by yourself."

Mary Ellen took a sip and smiled. "I love them. Don't get me wrong, you know I love wine, too—all kinds of wine—but I eat, sleep, think, breathe, work with wine all day every day. Everyone I know is in the wine business."

"I know that feeling." As she spoke, Molly looked up with a smile and nodded at someone behind Mary Ellen. No doubt the occupant of the corner booth had returned.

"I won't keep you." Much as she'd love to catch up with her friend, she could see Molly was busy. "I'd like the filet mignon and the parmesan truffle fries."

Molly grinned. "Good for you. Do you want me to bring out the bread rolls while you wait?"

Mary Ellen nodded. "Yeah, why not. If I'm going to blow it, I may as well go all out, right?"

Molly chuckled. "I have a friend who calls it calorie cycling. If your body gets used to being deprived, you stop losing weight, because your body's afraid it might starve. She says a good blowout every now and then just reassures your body that it's okay to keep shedding pounds."

"I like it. So, I'm not cheating or having a relapse or blowing it. I'm simply calorie cycling. And if that's the case, I might even need to have dessert."

Molly looked up again, and Mary Ellen felt bad for holding her up. Whoever was at the booth in the corner must be waiting. She wanted to turn around and apologize, but she knew there was no need. Molly left her with a smile, and Mary Ellen listened in as she spoke to the guy.

"Are you expecting company?"

"No. I'm here to enjoy my own company. I don't get chance very often."

Ooh. His voice sent shivers down Mary Ellen's spine. It was deep and sexy, but warm and friendly, too. It was one of those voices that sounded familiar, made you feel as though you knew its owner, even though you didn't.

Molly laughed, and the guy laughed with her, making Mary Ellen wonder why it was so funny that he didn't get chance to enjoy his own company much. She thought that was sad, not funny. She had lots of friends and a busy life, but she made sure she got time for herself, too. She'd go nuts if she didn't.

She dug her phone out of her purse. One of the things she enjoyed most was reading. She had a great book on the go right now and bringing herself out to dinner like this meant she could enjoy it, along with a great meal and no interruptions.

She smiled as Molly passed her on the way back to the kitchen. She was tempted to turn around and check out the guy with the sexy voice behind her, but there was no point. He probably wouldn't look anything like he sounded. She'd rather enjoy her imaginary version of him. It was a visual she could hang onto while she read—and she did. Soon she was lost in the story, and now the hero looked a lot like the way she imagined the guy in the corner booth did.

~ ~ ~

Antonio took a drink of his beer and smiled. It was good. He loved wine, but sometimes a guy just needed a beer. Tonight was one of those times. There was nothing wrong; in fact, his life was pretty damned good. He knew he lived a charmed life. He ran a great business, had great friends, and no shortage of female company. In fact, if he was honest with himself, he'd had more female company than he could handle lately. He'd always been a ladies' man. It was part of his identity. He was Antonio; he was successful; he was a winemaker, and he enjoyed the ladies. He took another slug of his drink. So why was he sitting here by himself drinking beer?

He shrugged and blew out a sigh. Nothing was wrong. It really wasn't. He was just getting tired of everything always being right. He never had to work too hard for anything. He might lead a charmed life—but that was losing its charm. He sighed again and noticed the blonde head at the next booth turn slightly at the sound. Hmm. He should maybe keep it down. He smiled. Or then again, maybe not? He could no doubt get her to turn all the way around if he wanted. He could strike up a conversation, invite her to join him. He could set himself the usual challenge—to take her home at the end of the evening. He smiled. It was hardly a challenge anymore. He'd done it so often. There was little thrill left in the chase. The odds were stacked in his favor. He was a good-looking guy, he was charming, women could tell he was wealthy, and once they learned he was in the wine business, it was pretty much all over. Or at least, they were all over him. He looked at the back of the blonde head and shrugged. No. He wanted an evening to himself.

He looked up as Molly returned to the blonde's booth with a Margarita. The two women chatted for a few moments then Molly left again. Antonio frowned. Was she a local? Molly seemed friendly with her. He furrowed his brow. Now that he thought about it, there was something familiar about the long blonde hair. He hoped she wasn't someone he knew. What did it matter? She had her back to him, and the server was heading toward him with his food. He was going to relax and enjoy his meal and forget about his surroundings.

He did enjoy his steak, but he couldn't quite forget about his surroundings. He watched as the server returned with the blonde's food. Filet, huh? In his experience, women who ate alone usually stuck to lighter fare.

After a little while, Molly came back to check on him. He smiled and nodded. "Everything's wonderful, Moll. As always."

She smiled and moved on to check on the blonde. "How is everything, Mary El?"

Antonio almost choked. Mary Ellen? He spluttered as the blonde head turned toward Molly and he caught a glimpse of the face. It was! Mary Ellen. Cameron's assistant. Chelsea's friend. He took a drink and cleared his throat.

Molly gave him a worried look, but he gave her a reassuring smile and dropped his gaze to his plate. He didn't want to attract Mary Ellen's attention. To his surprise, his heart was racing. What was he ... scared of her? He chuckled to himself at the thought. Perhaps he was. She was a beautiful woman, but she wasn't his type. Was that true? Physically, she was his type. She was gorgeous. Statuesque was the word that came to mind. She was voluptuous—great ass, great set, curves ... he drew in a deep breath. The woman had curves, the kind he'd love to get his hands on. He pursed his lips. He'd never tried. He liked to think it was merely because she was part of his social circle, and in a way, she was part of his family circle too. She worked with one cousin and was good friends with another cousin. He'd like to think that was the reason he'd never acted on his attraction to her, but that wasn't the whole reason. No. It was more to do with her personality. She was a no-nonsense kind of girl, from what he'd seen of her. She was capable and efficient. By Cameron's own admission, she played as big a part in the success of Hamilton-Groves as he did. She was smart, there was no doubt about it. Not just in her work either. She was witty. He blew out a sigh. She represented a different kind of challenge than he usually sought with a woman. With Mary Ellen, it wouldn't be a question of whether he could charm his way into her bed. He felt it'd be more a case of whether he could earn a place in it— he wasn't sure he could, so he'd never tried.

Antonio put his fork down at that realization. Was that why he was tired of female company lately? Because it was all too easy? Was he finding it all so meaningless because he'd deliberately been avoiding anything that could potentially be meaningful? He stared at the back of Mary Ellen's head. And was he ready to make a change? Should he attempt to talk to her?

Hell no!

He was so not ready for that.

He continued to shoot glances at her while he finished eating, pondering a question that had never occurred to him before about any woman. Was she out of his league?

He heard his cell phone ring and reached into his pocket, but it was silent. The familiar ring tone continued. It was coming from the booth ahead of him—Mary Ellen's. He listened as she answered. He shouldn't eavesdrop, but he couldn't help it.

"Hi, Mom. I'm doing okay, thanks. How are you and Dad? ... That's good ... Yes, I do know ... No. I'm not worried about it ... Mom, really. I'm fine."

Antonio had to wonder what her mom thought might be a problem.

"No. I didn't know he was coming. I didn't even know he was one of the candidates until yesterday ... No. I don't think he's here to make things up with me. I think he's here because it's a great opportunity."

Mary Ellen was quiet for a few moments, and when she spoke again, she was agitated. "Mom! Have you completely forgotten that David's married? I know we were engaged, but he dumped me, remember? I didn't fit the part. I'm not pretty enough; I'm not sweet and agreeable enough. Angela was a much better ticket to help him get where he wanted, so he unceremoniously dumped me for her. Why on earth would you think that he's come to Napa for me?"

Antonio felt bad. No way would Mary Ellen want him to hear any of this, but he could hardly get up and leave—for one thing, he was still eating, and for another, he was fascinated. This David guy must be a complete jackass. Mary Ellen was the kind of girl you married. She wasn't the kind of woman you dumped for an air-headed barbie—she was the kind you upgraded to when you were ready to man up. He looked up when she spoke again.

"Mom. I don't care. No, I didn't know he was divorced now, and no, I don't think this is a second chance with him. I've worked hard since then. I've worked on my career; I've worked on myself. I'm worth more than that. I might not be what a man's looking for, but I'm okay with me. I'd rather grow old alone than be somebody's second choice. I'm not going to be a fallback option, and I'm not going to accept crumbs."

Antonio swallowed, surprised by the lump that had formed in his throat. Her words were strong, and he could tell that she meant them, but there was a break in her voice. She was stating her truth, but he could hear her pain.

"I know, I know. I'm sorry, Mom. Listen. I've got to go, but I'll call you tomorrow, okay? Okay … love you … bye."

Antonio watched as she put her phone away. She leaned forward, her head bent. Was she crying? He hoped she wasn't crying. He swallowed. He had to do something. He couldn't stand to see her cry. No man should ever have been able to make her feel bad about herself. He had to tell her.

He bit the inside of his lip as he got up. He hesitated, looking around wildly. Maybe Molly would come? Girls knew how to help each other through, didn't they? No such luck. Molly was taking orders for a table of eight. She wasn't coming to the rescue. If anyone was going to be there to support Mary Ellen, it was going to have to be him. He walked toward her table. She was leaning her face in her hands. She didn't even look up. He couldn't tell if she was crying. He slid onto the bench across the table from her and waited. She still didn't look up.

"Are you all right?"

Her head shot up, and she met his gaze. For a second, he could see hurt and confusion in her eyes.

"Forgive me. I couldn't help overhearing your conversation."

Her eyes widened, and she covered her mouth with her hand. She still didn't speak, so he continued.

"I know it's none of my business, and it's not my place, but please, Mary Ellen, don't ever believe that you're not what a man is looking for. This David? He's not a man; he must be a complete asshole. If he left you for someone else, he doesn't know the worth of a woman. You think she was pretty? Believe me, she couldn't hold a candle to you. You're beautiful. You think she was sweet? A real man isn't looking for sweet. A real man is looking for strong, intelligent, witty. A real man is looking for a real woman, and that's what you are. Don't you ever believe otherwise, okay?"

Her expression had softened while he spoke. He knew it was a big risk, but he took it. He reached across the table and took hold of her hand. "You won't grow old alone. Someday someone will come along who'll want to earn your love. You deserve to be somebody's first choice. You'll be some lucky guy's one and only choice. Don't you ever doubt that, okay?"

Her eyes filled with tears. He squeezed her hand, and for a second, she squeezed back and nodded. Then she looked up. Molly was coming toward them.

"I have to go." She snatched up her purse and fled for the door.

"What's going on?" asked Molly when she reached the table.

Antonio shrugged. There was no way he could explain, nor would he want to. "She had to go. I'll get her tab."

Chapter Two

When Mary Ellen reached her apartment, she slammed the door behind her and leaned back against it. Her hands were shaking, and she was out of breath. That last part shouldn't be too much of a surprise, considering she'd practically run all the way back here. She took a few deep breaths and then pushed away from the door and went through to the bedroom to look at herself in the mirror. Her cheeks were flushed, and her eyes were shiny. She shrugged. It was good motivation to run more often.

She sat down on the end of the bed and looked herself in the eye. "Why are you so freaked out?" She shrugged again in response. She might not want to say it out loud, but she felt incredibly stupid. It was bad enough to hear that David was now divorced and that her mom thought he might have come to Napa to get back with her—and that she would want to. She shuddered. Is that all her mom thought she was worth? That she should be grateful for a second chance with a man who'd cast her aside without a second thought when he met someone who would be more useful to his career—oh, and who happened to have a tiny waist and huge boobs and giggled a lot? No. She wasn't going to take herself back down that slippery slope. She'd done the work, she'd gotten over it, she'd fought hard to regain her self-confidence, she wasn't going down that road again. She knew she deserved better than the way David had treated her.

But Antonio? Antonio Di-freaking-Giovanni? Her secret crush—the guy she'd spent more nights with than any other—not that he knew anything about that. He was her fantasy guy. His was the face she pictured when she … She felt her cheeks flush. But he was an asshole. An arrogant, superficial prick. Or at least, so she'd always thought. Ever since she'd first met him, she'd put him in the same league as David. A good-looking, successful guy—lovely on the outside, but not so lovely on the inside. He was superficial, the kind of person whose beauty was only skin deep.

She was mortified that he'd overheard her talking to her mom. She tried desperately to remember every word she'd said. What insight into her shame had she given him? She wouldn't want anyone on earth to have overheard that conversation—but him? She shook her head sadly. She'd have to find a new dream guy to fantasize about. There'd be no pleasure to be found in picturing his face now. It'd be too tainted with embarrassment.

She couldn't reconcile what he'd done—what he'd said—with the man she knew him to be. He was superficial. He was into money and beauty and easy sex. But the guy who'd sat down at her table—and taken hold of her hand, no less—that guy had been someone else entirely. He'd been caring and compassionate. She sighed. And still so damned gorgeous. All those things he'd said? He'd even told her she was beautiful. He'd said she was a real woman. Was he just so good at knowing what a woman needed to hear at any given point in time? Did it come from all those years of talking women into bed? No. She knew that wasn't it. He'd been so genuine; she'd been able to feel how much he cared. For a moment, she wondered what it would be like to have him care about her for real—not just momentary compassion—but if he cared about her like a boyfriend. She let out a little laugh. No. He might be a much more decent person than she'd ever given him credit for. It now made more sense that both Cameron and Chelsea thought so much of him—he'd probably be an awesome friend—but he didn't treat the women he got involved with that way. She knew that for a fact because he never kept them around for more than a date or two. And besides, it wasn't as if he would ever get involved with her. He was a fast mover with the ladies. She'd known him for years now, and he'd never shown a flicker of interest. If he'd found her attractive, she would have had her turn in his bed when she first came to Napa. She didn't doubt it.

She started at the sound of her phone ringing. She didn't want to talk to anyone, but it wasn't in her nature to ignore it. She dug it out of her purse. Chelsea's name flashed on the display. She smiled. If she had to speak to anyone right now, Chelsea would be the person she chose.

"Hey, girlfriend. What's up?"

"There's nothing up with me. Is there something up with you?"

Mary Ellen frowned, feeling defensive all of a sudden. "Why?"

"Because Grant and I just arrived at Molly's and she asked if I know what's going on with you."

"Tell her I'm sorry, I'll stop by in the morning and settle my bill. She doesn't need to worry that I did a runner on her."

"Cut the crap, Mary El. You know full well that's not what she's worried about. She said you seemed okay then you took a phone call that looked like bad news and then Antonio said something to you that sent you running out of here. I'm worried. What happened?"

"Nothing. Nothing at all. There's nothing to worry about. I'm fine, and I don't want to talk about it, okay?"

"No, that's not okay. In fact, that's so not okay, I'm going to have to come over and get it out of you."

"No! Didn't you say you and Grant just got to Molly's? Aren't you about to have dinner?"

"We were, but that's far less important. You usually tell me everything. So, you saying you don't want to talk about it freaks me out. I know it must be something horrible."

Mary Ellen blew out a sigh. "How about we have a girly night soon, and I'll tell you all about it? Right now, I want to have a bubble bath and an early night."

"Okay." Chelsea didn't sound convinced. "Tomorrow night."

"Tomorrow night it is. Now get off the phone and go have dinner with your man."

"Not until you tell me what Antonio did."

"There's nothing to tell."

"That's a lie."

Mary Ellen smiled and shook her head. "Okay, so it's a lie. But the truth is there's nothing I'm going to tell you before I see you tomorrow."

"Just tell me one thing?"

"No!"

"Fair enough. I'll see you tomorrow."

"Thanks, Chelsea. Just forget about it okay? It's nothing earth-shattering, there's nothing horrible going on, I promise. I'm fine. I was just a bit shaken up."

"Okay. If you say so. But tomorrow ..."

"Tomorrow I'll no doubt be ready to talk your ear off. Now, go."

"Okay, see you."

"Bye and say hi to Grant for me."

Mary Ellen hung up with a rueful smile. Chelsea was such a good friend—a fierce friend. She looked all cute and dainty; half the time she dressed like a fairy, but there was nothing weak about her. She was one determined little lady.

She got to her feet and went through to the bathroom to draw herself a bath.

~ ~ ~

Chelsea put her phone away and made a face at Grant.

"What did she say? Is she all right?"

"She says she's fine. She said nothing horrible happened, but she won't tell me what he did. I'm going to have dinner with her tomorrow and get it out of her."

Grant smiled. "I love the way you care about her so much. If she says she's okay, I'm inclined to believe her. I can't think of much that would shake Mary Ellen."

Chelsea pursed her lips. "Neither can I; that's what bothers me. I want to wring Antonio's neck!"

"Why?"

"Because Molly seemed to think he sent her running out of here."

Molly came back to the table with their drinks. "Did you talk to her?"

"Yeah. You know what she's like. She says she's fine. Tell me again what happened?"

Molly shrugged. "Maybe it was nothing, but the look on her face when she left … I don't know. She was sitting right here, and Antonio was in the booth behind. I didn't want to tell her he was there, because you know how she gets about him."

Chelsea nodded. "Yeah, that's what worries me."

Grant shook his head. "I don't get the deal with those two."

"There is no deal. Mary Ellen thinks he's gorgeous but only on the outside."

Grant chuckled. "Antonio thinks she's gorgeous, too."

Chelsea swung her head around to look at him. "He does?"

"Yeah!"

"But what …? Why …?" Chelsea shook her head. "I don't get it. Why's he never done anything about it? He never usually holds back if he likes a woman."

Grant shrugged.

"Maybe it's because she's one of us?" suggested Molly. "I mean, he gets around, but he's never dated anyone I know very well."

Chelsea made a face. "Yeah. Don't shit where you eat."

"Don't be too hard on him," said Molly. "At least it shows he has some values."

"Whatever. What did he do that sent her running out of here tonight? That's what I want to know."

"Maybe it wasn't even him. Like I said, she was on the phone for a few minutes. She looked upset, but I was taking a big order and couldn't get straight to her. Antonio came and sat here with her and said something and she got up and ran out. By the time I got here, all Antonio had to say was that she had to leave." Molly shrugged. "And he paid her check."

Chelsea drummed her fingers on the table. "I need to talk to him."

Grant smiled at her. "How about we track him down once we've had dinner? That way I get to eat, and you get a chance to calm down a little."

She smiled back. "Sorry, yeah, let's do that."

"Don't go yelling at him till you know the full story, will you?" said Molly. "I feel like I snitched on him and he might not even have done anything."

"Oh, he probably has," said Chelsea.

Grant shook his head at her. "Let's wait and see, can we?"

She drew in a big breath and then slowly blew it out. They were right. She got so protective of Mary Ellen. She was so strong and capable that everyone thought she was indestructible, but Chelsea knew better. She and Mary Ellen had become fast friends when Mary Ellen first arrived here, and Chelsea knew the heartbreak she'd clawed her way back from. She still didn't date much even now. She claimed it was because her life was full enough, but Chelsea worried that the real reason was because her heart was still too fragile. She had this huge crush on Antonio, and if he'd said something that hurt her, then he was going to be in deep trouble.

~ ~ ~

Antonio surveyed the dance floor from his seat at the bar. Like Molly's had been, it was busy in Muse for a Wednesday. The outdoor terrace was still half full of diners, and the dance floor was busy. There was a large party of women, most of whom were dancing, many of whom had already given him signals if he wanted to pick up on them. He didn't.

"Is everything all right?"

He looked up and smiled at the maître d'. "Everything's fine, Rodney."

Rodney nodded stiffly. He was a good man, if a little formal. Antonio was thrilled that he'd managed to headhunt him from one of the best restaurants in San Francisco when he opened Muse.

"Really. I'm okay." Antonio smiled again at the older man.

"If you insist, then I shan't ask again. However ..."

Antonio smiled at the way he left the invitation to talk hanging. Could he open up? Could he tell Rodney about what had happened this evening with Mary Ellen? No. He shook his head briefly. He didn't need to lay that on Rodney, even if he knew what had happened. What would he say? What could he say? "I appreciate it though."

Rodney nodded again and looked out at the dance floor. "It seems you have a rather nice selection of potential distractions on offer this evening."

"It would seem that way, wouldn't it?"

"Am I to understand you're not looking for a distraction?"

Antonio shook his head. "No. For what may be the first time in my life, I think what I need is reflection, not distraction."

The corners of Rodney's mouth turned up into what might be a smile. "Very well. I'll leave you be. When you're ready, remember I make a good sounding board."

"Thanks." Antonio smiled as he watched him walk away. Maybe he'd take him up on that offer when he figured out whatever it was he needed to talk about.

He watched the women dance for a few moments, hot bodies moving to the music, a couple of inviting looks thrown in his direction. It all left him cold. He should probably go home. He didn't even know why he'd come in here. Muse ran itself for the most part. He had a great management team in place, including Rodney.

He got to his feet and then sat back down again when he spotted Chelsea and Grant coming in. He loved them both, but he wished he'd left before they arrived. He wasn't in the mood for socializing.

He frowned as they approached. It didn't look like Chelsea was much in the mood for socializing either. His normally bright and cheery cousin wore a determined scowl and was heading straight for him. Grant followed in her wake, looking worried.

"Hey, Chels." He greeted her with a smile and wrapped her in a hug before she could launch into her offensive, giving Grant a *what's going on?* look over her shoulder as he did.

Grant held his palms up and gave him a helpless look.

He should have known better. No one could stop Chelsea when she got a bee in her bonnet. She was an unstoppable force, and it seemed that force was now directed at him.

She stepped back and scowled up at him. "Are you going to tell me?"

His heart sank. Damn. Had she spoken to Mary Ellen? "Tell you what?"

"What happened at Molly's tonight."

He lifted a shoulder and turned to wave the bartender over. He kind of hoped they didn't intend to stay for a drink, but he needed a minute to think about what he should say. "What have you heard?" he asked when he turned back around.

Chelsea glared at him. "What did you do?"

He smiled, knowing he looked much more confident than he felt. "I ate dinner, I had a beer."

"Antonio!" Chelsea's eyes flashed with anger. "You know damned well what I mean. What happened with Mary Ellen? Why was she so upset and why did she leave?"

He sure as hell wasn't about to tell them what he'd overheard. "Ah. Yes. I don't really know."

Chelsea continued to glare at him.

He glared back, but he couldn't keep it up. She stared him down. Damn her. Damn his soft Italian heart! He crumbled. "Okay, so she got a phone call that upset her. I felt bad for her, so I went and had a word with her, tried to cheer her up."

"And that was enough to send her running out of there?"

He shrugged. "Apparently."

Chelsea looked thoughtful. "What was the phone call about and what did you say to her?"

Antonio shook his head. "No. That's not my business to share. I think you should ask her."

"That just makes me think you're ashamed of what you did. Did you make a move on her because you thought she was upset and vulnerable?"

He sucked in a deep breath. He wasn't going to react. Sting as it might, it was a fair assumption, he supposed—given his track record. He shrugged. It didn't matter so much if Chelsea thought badly of him; what did matter was that he shouldn't go sharing Mary Ellen's business. "You should talk to her. If she wants to tell you what happened, I'm sure she will."

Chelsea glared at him again, apparently believing the worst. "I will." She turned on her heel and stalked out.

Grant stayed behind. "Are you okay?"

Antonio nodded.

"There's more to this than you're letting her think, right?"

He nodded again.

Grant smiled and grasped his shoulder. "Sorry, sometimes she gets a bit overzealous about protecting her people."

Antonio chuckled. "I know; I've known her all her life. It's one of the things I love about her. And when she calms down enough, I'll remind her that I'm one of her people, too. For now, I'm happy that she's looking out for Mary Ellen. Someone needs to."

Grant raised an eyebrow. "Is she okay?"

"Let's just say I think she could use a friend at the moment."

Grant looked at the door where Chelsea was waiting impatiently for him, then back at Antonio. "And would I be crazy if I guessed that you would like to be that friend?"

Antonio held his gaze for a long moment before he looked away and shrugged.

Chapter Three

"I was thinking." Mary Ellen dropped her gaze and fiddled with an imaginary speck on her skirt. "While you're interviewing this afternoon, I could get started on the quarterlies."

Cameron frowned. "Why would you do that? We don't start the quarterlies until next week, and besides, you're interviewing, too."

"I don't have to, though, do I? I mean, ultimately, the decision is yours."

"Look at me."

Mary Ellen pursed her lips. Damn. He was onto her.

"Mary Ellen." He sounded stern.

She reluctantly lifted her gaze to meet his.

"What's going on?

She made a face. There wasn't much she didn't tell Cameron. He was her boss, but he was also her friend. He was one of the people she admired most in the world. Maybe that was why she didn't want to admit what was going on. She knew he valued her, as a person and as his assistant. She didn't want him to think any less of her because of the whole David thing. What she really didn't want was for him to see David any differently because of her. If he thought David was the best man for the job, then he should hire him. She didn't want to get in the way of what was best for the business. "I don't know."

Cameron leaned his elbows on the desk and looked her in the eye. "Are you okay?"

Tears welled up in her eyes. Where the hell had they come from? She blinked them away angrily. "I'm fine!"

Cameron looked worried now. "You're obviously not. Do you want to tell me about it?"

"No. I don't. I just don't want to be part of the interviews this afternoon, that's all. I do everything you ever ask of me. Can I just go with a flat no, an unexplained no on this one?"

"Sure. If you don't want to do it, you don't have to. Are you sick? Do you want to go home?"

Mary Ellen thought about it. "I'm not sick, but you know what? I think I will go home at lunchtime. I'll take a half day."

"Okay. Whatever you need. Go now if you want."

"No. I've got plenty to be getting on with. And in case you'd forgotten, I need the Danson report from you."

Cameron smiled. "I haven't forgotten. I just need another hour on it."

"Good. If you do that now, I can take it home with me this afternoon."

"No. If you're going home, you're not going to work. Either have a rest and put your feet up, or go out and do something fun, but no work."

Mary Ellen smiled back. "Thanks, Cam."

"Are you sure you don't want to tell me what's up?"

She shook her head. She'd love to tell him, but she couldn't. "Nah, just put it down to hormones or something."

Cameron sat back in his chair, looking a little uncomfortable. "Ah. Okay. Sorry. I didn't think."

Mary Ellen laughed and got up. "No worries. I'll be in my office if you need me."

When she got to her desk, she stared at one of the photos on it. It was a group picture from a barbeque last summer. She stood between Cameron and Chelsea. Their parents were on one side, and Antonio and his brother Marcos were on the other. She loved that photo. It showed everything good about her life here. She peered at Antonio. She'd always loved that he was in the photo, but she'd never really looked at him before. At least, not beyond seeing the handsome face and sexy, muscular body. Now she looked into his eyes. Did they show any sign of the guy who'd spoken to her last night? He was smiling at the camera, his arm around his brother. No. There was nothing there to hint at a kind, compassionate heart, just a good-looking guy having a good time.

She needed to get some perspective back. He'd done a kind thing last night. He'd seen she was upset and had tried to make her feel better. He was a better person than she'd realized, but that was all, and that was the end of it. The next time she ran into him, she'd thank him, and perhaps in future, she wouldn't try so hard to stay out of his way, but that was all. His act of kindness would cost her the guy she fantasized about—that guy had no personality or soul, he was just a handsome face with a hot body. Perhaps he'd be able to fill a new role as just a decent guy she knew. She chuckled. Perhaps she should think of him now as a tart with a heart.

Last night was done with. Hopefully, after the interviews today, she'd be able to put the whole episode behind her. She had to believe that Cameron wouldn't think David was the right man for the job. He was good at what he did, she knew that, but he wasn't a good human being. She had to trust that Cam would see that and hire someone else. If he didn't … Well, she'd just have to cross that puddle when it rained. If it rained. Big if there. For now, she was going to finish up with the report she'd been working on, then she was going to take herself home for the afternoon. She'd rather stay here and work, but it was best if she wasn't around. She didn't want to risk running into David if she could help it. Maybe she should hit the treadmill and do penance for last night's dinner.

~ ~ ~

Antonio stared at his computer. He couldn't concentrate this morning. He couldn't stop thinking about last night—about Mary Ellen. He could still hear the pain in her voice. It bothered him. No one should be able to make her feel that way.

He kept rolling it around in his head. What was her history with this David guy? She must have loved him. Who was he? What was he doing here? What had she said? She hadn't known he was coming to Napa. He was one of the candidates—candidates for what? She didn't think he'd come here for her. She thought he'd come because it was a great opportunity. What was? He wished he could ask Cameron, but he wouldn't. Cameron and Mary Ellen were close. Cam thought the world of her, and even if he did know the story, he probably wouldn't tell—and he'd want to know why it mattered to Antonio. What could he tell him when he didn't know himself?

Antonio drummed his fingers on the desk. He should forget about it, forget about her. He'd overheard what should have been a private conversation. He'd done his best to make her feel a little better afterward. That was it. End of story. Nothing to do with him. He got to his feet. He needed to go down to check in with the sales team on the big Ellery order.

He was almost to the door when a thought struck him, stopping him dead in his tracks. Cameron! He was interviewing. He was looking for a new sales director. Surely to God, this David character wasn't one of the candidates for the position? Cameron wouldn't do that to Mary Ellen, would he?

He picked up his phone and dialed his cousin's cell phone.

"Antonio! What's up?"

"Hey." He didn't know what to say. How could he ask anything without explaining everything? "Hey, Cam. How're things?"

"Busy. If this is just social, do you mind if I call you back tonight? I'm kind of busy, interviewing for the new sales director."

"I know, that's what I was calling about." He took a deep breath. He could bluff. He wouldn't normally give it a second thought. "Isn't David one of the candidates?"

"David Sterling?"

Antonio waved his hand in the air. How the hell would he know what the guy's last name was? "Yeah." He smiled as he spoke, knowing it would come through in his voice. "David Sterling. He used to work at Kendall, right?"

"I don't think so. Though at this point I could be getting him mixed up with one of the other candidates. Why? Do you know him?"

"Only by reputation." That wasn't a lie.

"Do you think he'd be a good fit here? He's one of my top two at this point."

Antonio pursed his lips. He didn't even know if this David Sterling was Mary Ellen's David. He could hardly go scuppering the guy's chance at a great career move. "Not my place to say, Cam. You know that. What does Mary Ellen think?"

"This is so weird."

"What is?"

"I have no clue what she thinks, which isn't like her, and instead of helping me with the interviews, she's taken the afternoon off. Now you're asking about her when you never normally speak her name out loud. Is something going on?"

Antonio's heart was racing. He couldn't lie to his cousin, but it wasn't his place to explain what was going on—or even what he thought was going on. "I don't know, Cam. I'm sorry. I'm sticking my nose into business I know nothing about."

Cameron sighed. "You know you're going to have to explain this to me, right?"

"Yup."

"And you know I don't have time right now."

"Yup. So, I guess you'll just have to meet me for a drink this evening."

"I guess I will, and in the meantime, I'll have to try to not let my curiosity get in the way when I interview David."

"I guess you will. Muse at six?"

"Okay. But this had better be good."

Antonio hung up. He didn't relish the thought of explaining himself to Cameron. He didn't even really know why he was doing this, but for some reason, he felt good about it.

~ ~ ~

Mary Ellen paced the apartment after she buzzed Chelsea into the building. She was kind of dreading this, while at the same time part of her was looking forward to telling Chelsea about last night. She hadn't even told her about David being here yet so it would be a relief to talk about that, at least.

She went to the front door and opened it just as Chelsea was emerging from the elevator. "Hey, you."

"Don't hey me." Chelsea scowled at her. "Pour us a glass of something and tell me what happened last night."

Mary Ellen laughed and led her through to the kitchen where she poured them each a glass of wine. "Don't be mad at me, I just couldn't process it all, and I didn't want to ruin your evening with Grant. It wasn't urgent or anything."

Chelsea wandered back through to the living room. "What wasn't? I was worried about you. Molly said you seemed upset by your phone call, and when I talked to Antonio, he wouldn't tell me a thing. I asked if he tried making a move on you, and he didn't deny it. Did he?"

"You talked to Antonio?" Mary Ellen's heart raced. Had he told her about David?

"Of course, I did. You wouldn't tell me what had happened, so I went to see him."

"And what did he say?"

"Nothing. He wouldn't tell me a thing, said it wasn't his place. He said I should talk to you."

Mary Ellen smiled. Wow. He really was a much more decent human being than she'd thought.

Chelsea gave her a hard stare. "What's the smile for?"

Mary Ellen grinned. "He's a good guy, really, isn't he?"

Chelsea smiled back. "He is. I've always told you that. So, why do you believe it all of a sudden?"

Mary Ellen blew out a sigh, but still couldn't quite wipe the smile off her face. "Okay. I'd better start at the beginning, and then you'll understand why I was so upset and why I'm so pleasantly surprised by him. See, what I haven't told you is that David is in town."

"David? You mean your David?"

Mary Ellen nodded. "David Sterling, the man I was engaged to. He's not mine, and I don't believe he ever was, but yes, that David."

"Wow! Why? What's he doing here and what's Antonio got to do with it?"

"My mom called while I was having dinner because she found out he was here, and she thought it was a chance for me to get back with him." She shook her head sadly. "As if! I got upset, I admit it. I think it was mostly because I thought my mom understood how badly he hurt me, and I thought she might care about me, but all she was thinking was that I might have another chance with him since he's divorced now."

Chelsea shook her head. "Your mom thought that? After what he did to you?"

"Yeah. It upset me, but she means well. She just wants to see me all married and settled down, and apparently, she thinks David was my one and only chance."

"Don't. I'm sure she doesn't think that at all. But explain the rest. Why is David here—has he come to see you? And what's Antonio got to do with any of it?"

"Okay. This is what I haven't told you yet. David is here because he's interviewing for the sales director job."

Chelsea frowned. "What? Why? Why would Cameron even consider him?"

Mary Ellen dropped her gaze.

"You haven't told him, have you?" demanded Chelsea.

Mary Ellen shook her head.

"Why?"

She looked up. "Because it's about finding the best person for the job. It's not about my personal life; it's about the company."

"Oh, for God's sake, Mary El. That's crazy! Do you realize how much of the success of Hamilton-Groves depends on you? How much Cameron depends on you? I can tell you right now that David is not the right person for the job because him being there would upset you. And that would be bad for the company. You've got to tell Cameron."

Mary Ellen shrugged. "Maybe. I've been hoping that it would resolve itself. I thought that when Cam interviewed him, he'd see through him. I thought, you know, it'd all iron itself out without me doing anything."

"When's the interview?"

"This afternoon."

"And what did Cam think?"

"He's taken him through to the final three."

"Then you have to tell him."

Mary Ellen took a sip of her wine but didn't say anything.

"And I still don't get where Antonio comes into any of it."

"Antonio overheard me talking to my mom. He was sitting right behind me; it wasn't his fault. I was so embarrassed when I realized that he'd overheard everything I said. I told her I'd rather grow old alone than be David's second choice and I talked about how he dumped me for someone prettier and sweeter and ..." She shook her head. "He overheard all of it."

Chelsea frowned. "And what did he say to you?"

Mary Ellen couldn't help the smile that spread across her face. "He was so sweet, Chelsea. He told me David must be an asshole, and that I'm a real woman and I'm beautiful and that I shouldn't be someone's second choice because someday I'll be someone's one and only choice. He was so damned sweet."

Chelsea put both her hands on her heart and grinned. "Aww, bless him. He is a big sweetie, really. I feel bad for giving him a hard time now, but I thought he was the one who'd upset you somehow."

Mary Ellen shook her head. "No, the only thing that upset me was embarrassment that he'd heard everything, and I was shocked that he was so kind and caring. He wasn't the guy I thought he was."

Chelsea rolled her eyes. "I've been telling you that for years."

"I know, I know."

"So, what are you going to do?"

"There's nothing I can do. I mean, it's not as though he likes me or anything; he was just being kind."

Chelsea raised her eyebrows. "I meant about David, but I find it interesting that you're more concerned about Antonio."

"Oh." Mary Ellen wanted to make an excuse, but there was no point. She gave her friend a rueful smile. "I want Cam to hire whoever he thinks is best."

"Fair enough, but don't make him choose blind. He needs to know who David is, and I'm sure that will affect his decision. He won't want David around if he knows how it will affect you."

Mary Ellen nodded. She knew Chelsea was right. She'd been trying to bury her head in the sand, but it wouldn't be fair to Cameron to let him hire David and then find out the history there.

"It's okay. If you don't want to tell him. I will."

"No. You can't blackmail me into it that way. I'll tell him myself tomorrow."

"Good. And what about Antonio?"

"What about him?"

Chelsea grinned. "Well. It's no great secret that you've had this crush on him. Now that you can finally see what a good guy he is, are you going to go out with him?"

"Ha! Aren't you forgetting that he gets a say in this too?"

"No. He likes you. I think it's time the two of you finally went out."

"He does not. If he liked me, he'd have hit on me years ago—and you know damned well I wouldn't have been able to resist. I'd have fallen right into his bed just like the rest of them."

"So, what's stopping you now?"

Mary Ellen shook her head. "He was just being kind." And if he really did like her? Would she still want her turn in his bed?

Chelsea sighed. "Maybe he's the fling you need right now. He could help you past this whole David episode. Boost you back up."

Mary Ellen smiled. Wouldn't that be something?

Chapter Four

"Will you and Mr. Hamilton be eating this evening?"

"No." Antonio smiled at Rodney. "We're just meeting for a quick drink. We won't need the table for more than an hour."

"Very well."

Antonio spotted Cameron making his way through the bar and smiled. He'd decided he was going to be completely honest with him.

Cameron made to shake his hand when he reached him. Antonio grinned and pulled him in for a hug.

Cameron grinned back. "It's good to see you, too. I can't stay for long. Piper's getting back from Phoenix tonight and I haven't seen her since Monday morning."

"Don't worry, I won't keep you. And give her my love, won't you? I bet she hates being away with all the wedding planning you two must be doing."

Cameron laughed. "I think she's glad to be away. She's not much of a planner."

Antonio raised an eyebrow.

"It works well for us. I enjoy it, and she doesn't have to deal with the stress. But that's not what we're here to talk about. What's going on? What's your interest in David Sterling?"

Antonio shrugged. He felt a little embarrassed. Was it really his place to tell Cam that he shouldn't hire a guy? He knew full well that it wasn't his place to talk about Mary Ellen's private business. "Let's get a drink first." He beckoned to the waiter who had been hovering since Cam came in.

Once he'd gone, Cam jerked his head toward the bar. "Am I right in thinking that you'd rather talk about him than to him?"

Antonio followed his gaze, not understanding. "To who?"

Cam frowned. "David. He's standing right there at the end of the bar."

"Oh." Antonio scowled at the guy. So, he was the one who'd broken Mary Ellen's heart? It gave him a little hope. If that was her type, then he might be in with a chance. David was good-looking. He was tall and dark with an olive complexion. He looked like he must have some Latin blood.

"Why do you look like you want to kill him?"

He turned back to Cameron who was giving him a puzzled look. "What? No! I ... I just. Well ... Oh, you know what? Fuck it. I'm going to tell you. But you can't tell Mary Ellen, okay?"

Cameron looked baffled. "What the hell is going on? What do you know about Mary El that I don't? That just seems so unlikely to me that it's hard to believe, and what does David have to do with any of it?"

Antonio blew out a sigh and explained the events of the night before. He glossed over what he'd heard Mary Ellen say, and he glossed over what he'd told her afterward, but he gave Cam the basic idea of what had happened. "So, you see. That guy." He jerked his head at David. "Broke Mary Ellen's heart and I don't think you should hire him."

Cameron nodded. "Are you sure it's him? Are you sure that's the David she was talking about? She's never mentioned him before and she sure as hell hasn't said anything about knowing him while we've been going through the selection process."

Antonio shrugged. "That's why I feel like an asshole. I'm sharing a secret that I shouldn't even know. And no. I'm not even sure that he's the guy. I put two and two together, and I might be coming up with five. But come on, Cam, what are the odds?"

Cameron nodded and looked back over at David. "I think it has to be him. And if it is, then I don't want him on the team. He might be great for the job, but if it'd upset Mary Ellen, then it's just not worth it."

"Do you think he would be great for the job?"

"I don't know. I told you at lunchtime he was in my top two. When you look at his resumé he's perfect. He interviewed well, and he should be a good fit, but I didn't quite click with him. He said all the right things, he was impressive, but I don't know. There was just some disconnect. I thought it was just me, but now I'm more inclined to trust my gut."

Antonio grinned. "Good."

"Why's it so important to you?"

Antonio froze. He'd been so happy that David wouldn't get the chance to worm his way back into Mary Ellen's life that he hadn't stopped to think about why. He shrugged. "Mary Ellen is a good person. You couldn't do what you do without her. I'd hate to see things get messed up. That's all."

"That's all?" Cameron held his gaze, the hint of a smile playing on his lips.

Antonio stared back at him. Damn. "Last night, Chelsea stared me down. Now you're doing it! I don't know what to tell you.

Last night, hearing her talk, she was upset, she was hurt. I just
… It hurt me for her, you know? She deserves better than
some guy dumping her and making her feel bad about herself."
Cameron nodded. "She does. She deserves the best."
"Exactly."
"And you've always seen yourself as the best, right?"
Antonio smiled. "I have, but I'm not sure I'm that good."
Cameron chuckled. "For some reason, I get the idea we're
going to find out."
Antonio thought about it. What was he going to do? Should he
ask Mary Ellen out? Would she say yes if he did? He looked at
Cameron and nodded. "It might take me a little while."
Cameron smiled. "It's already taken you years longer than I
thought it would."
"What do you mean?"
"I mean, I always thought you and Mary Ellen might get
together someday."
"You did?"
"I did. It makes sense somehow."
Antonio swallowed. If Cam thought it was a possibility, then
maybe it wasn't as crazy as he'd been telling himself it was.

~ ~ ~

Mary Ellen checked the clock above her desk. She rarely
noticed the time when she was at work. She loved her job,
loved being here, but today she just wanted out. It was Friday,
and she wanted the weekend to hurry the hell up and start.
Despite what she'd told Chelsea last night, despite the fact that
she knew she should, she hadn't said anything to Cameron
about David. He'd had to get straight on a call with the New
York office when he arrived and had spent most of the
morning putting out fires. She'd thought she'd have to tell him

about David when they conducted the final interviews, but Cam hadn't even invited her to sit in. She'd stayed holed up here in her office and was dreading he might walk in any moment with David at his side, introducing him as the new sales director. She blew out a sigh. She should have told him. If he did hire David, it'd be her own fault, and she'd just have to make the best of a bad situation.

She jumped at the sound of a knock on the door. Cam stuck his head around it and smiled. "Are you okay?"

She nodded and waited, convinced that when the door opened fully, David would be standing there.

He wasn't. Cam came in and closed the door behind him.

"How did the interviews go?"

He nodded. "They went well. I think you're going to get along with our newest team member."

Mary Ellen nodded. She would. She'd have to. "Who did you go with?"

Cam gave her a rueful smile. "Don't worry, not David."

"Oh! You knew?"

He nodded. "I did. I wish you'd told me yourself."

Mary Ellen shrugged. "I didn't want my stupid personal stuff to get in the way of whatever's best for the business."

"It's not stupid stuff. Don't say that. You have a history with the guy."

"I do, but that shouldn't matter."

"Maybe it shouldn't, but it would have. Anyway. It's irrelevant because he wasn't the best man for the job. I think Paul's a much better fit with us and with the company values. He's in with HR at the moment, but they're going to bring him back here when they're done."

Mary Ellen smiled and sighed a big sigh of relief. "Good. I liked him, and you're right, I think he'll fit in well."

"Are you doing anything straight after work? I thought we could round up some of the team and take him for a welcome drink."

"That's a great idea. I'll see who's around." She picked up her phone to dial the sales office. "Connor and Lyle just got back from Bakersfield. They're always up for a drink after work, and they should meet their new boss."

"Great. I'll see who I can find. Tell them Muse at five-thirty."

Mary Ellen's throat went dry. "Muse?"

Cameron grinned. "Yeah. Is that a problem?"

She shook her head. It shouldn't be. It might be Antonio's wine bar, but he wouldn't be there at five-thirty, would he? And even if he was, all she needed to do was thank him for being kind to her the other night. That was all. And then she could put the whole episode behind her.

She realized Cameron had stopped with his hand on the door. He was watching her intently.

"What?"

He shook his head with a smile. "Just making sure you're okay."

"Why wouldn't I be?"

"You never told me a thing about David."

"Oh." And there she'd been thinking he was onto her about Antonio! "He's the past. I should have said something when I knew he was in the running for the job, but ..." She shrugged. "It all worked out okay, didn't it?"

"It did. Okay, let's round up the troops and go celebrate."

~ ~ ~

Rodney greeted Antonio with a questioning smile when he arrived at Muse.

Antonio grinned at him. "This may be the third evening I've been here this week, but it's been an unusual week, and technically it's the weekend now."

Rodney smiled. "It is. Does this mean you're back to your usual routine?"

Antonio knew what he meant. The usual Friday night saw him having dinner here and leaving with a woman. "No. I'm breaking with routine. I'm going to eat, and then I'm going home—alone."

Rodney raised an eyebrow.

"Don't look at me like that. I am."

"Very well. Your table is available if you want to eat now. However, Mr. Hamilton is here with a group of his colleagues. They're on the patio upstairs, if you feel like socializing."

Antonio pursed his lips. Would Mary Ellen be amongst Cameron's colleagues? And if she were, would he want to join them—or to stay away?

"Do I sense uncertainty?" asked Rodney.

Antonio nodded.

"This is an unusual week." Rodney gave him a knowing smile.

Antonio laughed. "I feel like I should be calling you Sensei or Master or something! It feels like you know what's going on with me better than I do. Care to share?"

Rodney tried to look innocent, but he couldn't pull it off. He smiled and gripped Antonio's shoulder. "I've seen this coming for a while. You're outgrowing the life you've been living. I'm eager to see what you will do—where you go from here."

Antonio smiled back. "Me too, but at this point, I don't have a clue what I'm doing or where I'm going."

"You'll figure it out. Go slowly. Tread lightly."

Antonio laughed. "That's not much help. Do you have anything more concrete for me?"

Rodney smiled. "Right now, I'd suggest you join your cousin."

"Why?"

"Because I was intrigued by the look on your face when I told you he and his colleagues are here."

Antonio smiled through pursed lips. "Damn, you're good. Was there a blonde amongst his colleagues?"

Rodney smiled. "Ah! Mary Ellen? Yes, she's here. And in that case, I strongly suggest you join them."

Antonio chuckled. "Yes, Master." As he made his way out to the terrace, he noticed that his palms were sweaty. He drew in a deep breath—his heart was racing, too. Why? What was he afraid of? When he spotted her, he understood. It wasn't fear that was making him react that way. It was Mary Ellen, it was … what? Excitement? Attraction? He didn't know which, but he liked it, whatever it was. She was so damned beautiful. She was sitting side-on to him so he could study her profile as he approached without her noticing. His smile faded as he looked at the guy she was talking to. He didn't recognize him, and he looked a little too interested.

Cameron got to his feet. "Antonio. I didn't think we'd see you here this early."

Mary Ellen turned her head slightly but looked away again quickly.

Antonio smiled at Cameron. "It's Friday. It looks like we all felt the need to escape the office early." He looked around the group, nodding at Connor and Lyle from the sales team, smiling at others he didn't know so well. Finally, he was looking directly at Mary Ellen. Her cheeks flushed, and she gave him a brief nod. Damn. She didn't look pleased to see him. If anything, she looked irritated. For all the time he'd spent thinking about her since Wednesday night, he hadn't dedicated much thought to whether she might be angry at him for listening to her conversation. He smiled brightly and nodded back. "Mary Ellen."

"Antonio."

Antonio looked at Cameron. He didn't know what to do. And that wasn't a position he was accustomed to being in.

Cameron grinned. "Paul. I'd like you to meet Antonio Di Giovanni. Antonio, I'm sure you'll be very happy to meet our new sales director, Paul Stevens."

Antonio was thrilled. "Paul. It's a pleasure to meet you."

The guy stood to shake his hand. "You, too. It's an honor. I love your wines." He smiled at Cam. "Though, of course, not quite as much as Hamilton-Groves wines."

Cameron laughed. "Of course not."

Antonio's heart sank as Mary Ellen got up and excused herself. Was she going to the bathroom? Was she leaving because of him? He hoped not. He shot a look at Cameron, but he just lifted a shoulder and guided Paul toward Connor and Lyle to join their conversation.

Antonio stared at the doorway through which Mary Ellen had just disappeared. Had she gone? There was only one way to find out. He set out after her.

~ ~ ~

Mary Ellen stared at herself in the mirror in the bathroom. "Not cool, Mary El. Not cool," she berated herself. Why had she gotten up and walked away? She'd promised herself that if they ran into Antonio, she would be cool. She was going to thank him graciously for his kindness the other evening, and that would be an end to it. And what had she done? She'd gone bright red when he spoke to her and then as good as sprinted out of there the first chance she got.

She shook her head and fished her lipstick out of her purse. Now she had to go back out there. That was even worse. She washed her hands just to kill some time. As she was drying them, there was a knock on the bathroom door. A knock? That was weird. The door wasn't locked, there were three stalls in here. Maybe it was the cleaner? It came again, louder this time.

"Mary Ellen?"

Her hand flew up to cover her mouth. It was him. Antonio. She stared at the door, then came to her senses. "Yes?"

The door swung open, and he came inside. Her heart pounded in her chest at the sight of him. It always did, he was just that handsome, but normally she was able to observe him from afar. His attention was never focused on her. It was right now. He was standing there—in the ladies' room, no less—towering over her, staring down into her eyes. She looked up into his. His big, brown, beautiful eyes. They melted her insides, but she couldn't afford to think about that.

"Please forgive me?"

She cocked her head to one side. "What for?"

He smiled, and all she could focus on were his full, beautiful lips.

"For everything, for anything. I shouldn't have listened in the other night. I shouldn't have said anything to Cameron. I shouldn't have done a lot of things, but I only did them because I care."

Mary Ellen's mind spun. "What did you tell Cameron?" That was the only reasonable question she could come up with.

His smile faded. "He didn't tell you?"

She shook her head.

"Oh."

"Tell me what?"

"That I told him about David."

"You did?"

He nodded. "I'm sorry."

She stared at him for a long moment. She couldn't be mad at him. She couldn't be mad at Cameron. The only person she should really be mad at over the whole David episode was herself. She should have told Cam from the outset, and there would never have been a problem.

"Please don't be angry with me."

She chuckled. "I'm not. Part of me wants to be, but I'm not. You meant well, didn't you?"

He nodded vigorously. "I heard you. I heard how you felt. There's no way you should have to be around that man. Cameron didn't know, and I knew he would want to. I know it wasn't my place, but I care."

"You do?" What was he saying? Did he mean he cared about her? Or just that he cared in general, that he was a caring person? He stepped toward her. Oh, God! Was he going to kiss her? Did she want him to? Hell yeah, she did!

"Oh! I'm sorry."

Mary Ellen sprang away from Antonio as the door opened behind him. Natasha from the office stood there looking shocked—it wasn't every day you found a handsome Sicilian when you walked into the ladies' room.

Antonio smiled at her as if she were the one out of place. "That's okay, we were just leaving." He held the door for Mary Ellen and gestured for her to go out ahead of him.

When they were out into the hallway, he laughed, and she had to laugh with him. "I'm sorry again. I seem to be screwing this up every time I turn around."

The laughter died in her throat. "Screwing what up?"

He put a hand on her shoulder, sending shivers chasing each other down her spine and making her knees want to buckle under her. "Asking you out. Will you have dinner with me? Tonight, tomorrow, whenever you want?"

She looked up into his eyes. Was he messing with her? No. It didn't look like it. He looked as concerned and caring as he had when he talked to her on Wednesday. Maybe it was just part of his play to get a woman into bed—and if it was, it was working. She nodded. "Okay."

"Tonight?"

She nodded again. Why not? She'd waited years for her turn in his bed. Why wait any longer? They both knew what it was about, why not just get on with it? "Later. I need to hang out with the team first."

He smiled. There went those full lips, curving up at the corners and making her heart race again at the thought that later they'd be touching her skin—all over. "I'll let you get back to it. I'll be here when you're done."

She smiled. "Okay." As she turned away from him, he touched her shoulder, and she turned back. He lowered his head; he was going to kiss her. She closed her eyes but didn't get what she expected. He closed his hand around the back of her neck and gently planted a kiss on top of her head. "I can't wait."

She did her best to walk steadily back out to the terrace to rejoin the others, but she felt a little wobbly and had a feeling she might look as if she was walking on air.

Chapter Five

Antonio checked his watch. How long would it take? It'd already been an hour since Mary Ellen went back to join her colleagues. Patience wasn't one of his strengths. Once he made a decision, he preferred to move swiftly. He wasn't in the driver's seat here though. It was all up to Mary Ellen. At least she'd said yes—and she was attracted to him. He knew plenty about women, and the way she'd reacted to him in the bathroom had made it plain. She was physically attracted to him.

Normally, that would be all he needed to know. If he was going to have dinner with a woman and she was attracted to him, he knew how the evening would go—and how it would end. That wasn't the case with Mary Ellen. He wasn't on a mission to get her into bed, at least not yet, not tonight. He shifted in his seat. The thought of getting her into bed had the interest stirring in his pants. If he started to think about her body, about getting his hands on her and … Damn. He hadn't allowed himself to think of her that way before. He'd believed there was no point. She wouldn't be interested. But she was. What was he going to do with it? He wanted to get to know her, as a person, not just as a piece of ass. He couldn't deny he wanted to get his hands on her ass—on every inch of her creamy skin. His hands, his tongue … he shook his head. He wasn't supposed to be taking it in that direction. She wasn't the kind of girl who'd sleep with him on a first date. And, gorgeous as she was, it wasn't just her body that interested him. If all he wanted was a hot body, he could find one to take home any night of the week. What he was interested in was the woman, Mary Ellen. He wouldn't find another like her in a million years; he already knew that. She was special. The question was, would she find him special, too?

He looked up as Cameron came through the bar. "I'm heading home."

"Okay. Have a great weekend."

"Thanks. You too." Cameron smiled at him. "Mary Ellen's still here."

"I know."

"How?"

"Because I asked her to stay and have dinner with me."

Cameron chuckled. "Awesome. I hope it goes well." Cameron's smile faded, and Antonio turned to follow his gaze to where David Sterling had just taken a seat at the other end of the bar. "I thought he would have left town by now."

Antonio frowned. "Me too. I should go out there and find Mary Ellen. I don't think she'd enjoy running into him."

"Too late." Cameron was looking at the entrance from the terrace where Mary Ellen was standing, frozen in place, staring at David.

Antonio's fist clenched at his side as he watched David get up and go to her.

Cameron put a hand on his arm. "Don't you think you should give them a minute?"

"No. If you were waiting for your date to meet you for dinner, would you sit and watch while some other guy made a move on her?" He didn't wait for Cameron's reply, but strode toward Mary Ellen, with just one thought running through his mind. *That's the asshole who hurt her. He's not going to get chance to again.*

"Mary Ellen." David reached her moments before Antonio. "It's so good to see you. I hoped I'd run into you before now."

Mary Ellen's face gave nothing away; she wore a polite mask. "It's been a busy week."

"Will you have dinner with me?"

Antonio held his breath, wondering how she would answer. She noticed him and met his gaze. The mask slipped, and she seemed to be pleading with him to save her. At least, that's how he read it. He stepped forward and slid his arm around her waist. "Hey, bella. There you are." He dropped a kiss on top of her head and hugged her into his side. "How was your day, honey?"

She looked up at him, her eyes wide. She was either angry or shocked. He couldn't tell which, and it was too late now. He couldn't help it. He leaned down and dropped a kiss on her lips, before finally acknowledging David. "Hi. You must be Paul? Congratulations."

David frowned, and Mary Ellen dug her elbow into his ribs. "No. This is David. David Sterling."

Antonio held the guy's gaze for a moment. He couldn't tell the guy what he thought of him, but he tried to convey his feeling with the look he gave him. "You're David? Wow." He smiled. "I guess all I can say is thank you."

"Thank you?" David looked puzzled, and so did Mary Ellen.

Antonio tightened his arm around Mary Ellen's waist. "For setting her free so I could find her."

David didn't know what to say to that. He looked at Mary Ellen, then back at Antonio and nodded. "Yeah. It was good to see you again, Mary El." He turned around and left.

Antonio kept his arm around Mary Ellen, wondering what kind of reaction he was going to get. She didn't pull away from him as he looked down into her eyes. Her head was cocked to one side. She looked puzzled but not angry. Best of all, she still hadn't moved away from him. She felt so good, tucked into his side with her full breast grazing his arm. He didn't want to explain himself, so instead, he waited for her to speak first.

"Do you want to tell me what that was all about?"

He lifted a shoulder and gave her a sheepish grin. "I thought it might be better if he left."

She nodded. "Yeah, but was it for your sake or mine?"

He smiled. "Honestly? Both."

She chuckled and nodded. "You're quite a character, aren't you?"

He grinned. "I like to think so."

She stepped away from him, and he immediately missed her warmth and wanted to pull her back into his arms. He might have, until he noticed Cameron approaching.

"I thought you'd gone home?" He tried for the offensive before Cam could ask what the hell was going on.

Cameron laughed. "What and miss this little show? No way." He turned to Mary Ellen. "What's going on?"

There was a touch of color in her cheeks as she shrugged, but she was smiling. "I have no idea. You'd better ask your cousin that one. I think he sees me as a damsel in distress and just came to my rescue."

Cameron chuckled. "And you didn't want to be rescued?"

Mary Ellen looked up at Antonio. "I did. I'm very grateful."

Antonio breathed a sigh of relief.

"Good. I'm going home then," said Cameron. "You guys have fun."

Antonio watched him go, then turned back to Mary Ellen. "You heard the man, and he is your boss, you have to do as he says."

"What, have fun?" She smiled. "Well, if Cam says I must, then I'd better try."

Antonio noticed Rodney hovering and beckoned him over. "Is everything all right?"

"Yes. Your table is ready whenever you are."

"Thanks." Antonio offered Mary Ellen his arm. "Shall we?"

She grinned and slipped her arm through his. "I'd love to."

~ ~ ~

Once they were seated, Mary Ellen looked across the table at Antonio and then looked around the restaurant. She blew out a big sigh and turned to take in the beautiful view. This was Antonio's table. The best in the house, with the best view of the valley.

"Is everything okay?"

She tore her eyes away from the view to look at him and nodded. "Yes. It just seems so strange to be sitting here with you. I mean, this is your table, your wine bar. You're Mr. Popular. I'm more used to observing this scene than being a part of it."

He frowned. "What do you mean?"

She chuckled. "I don't know. We've known each other for so long, but we've never really known each other at all. I'll be honest, I thought you were an asshole."

He put his hand over his heart and gave her a hurt look.

She laughed. "Don't. You know exactly what I mean. Don't you?"

He nodded. "I'm afraid I do. I'm grateful that now I get the chance to prove to you that that's not all I am."

"You already have. The other night, at Molly's? Thank you. That was so sweet of you."

He nodded. "I'm sorry I overheard, but I had to say something. I could hear how hurt you were. I … I'm sorry."

"I'm not. I appreciate it. And thank you for getting rid of him tonight."

Antonio smiled. Did he have to keep doing that? He had such a sexy smile. It made her want to skip dinner and get straight to what happened afterward. She couldn't wait, but at the same time, she wanted to enjoy the whole evening. She wasn't a fool. She knew it'd just be one night, and she wanted to make the most of every minute with this new Antonio. He was turning out to be a great guy.

"I told you, it was for my sake as well as yours. I didn't want him to upset you, and I didn't want him to hold you up. I want you all to myself."

The way he said it sent shivers down her spine. She met his gaze. His big brown eyes bore into hers. Was he thinking the same as she was? Did he want to skip dinner and just get on with it, too? If he did, he was hiding it well. He still looked like he cared, not like he just wanted into her panties. But maybe that was part of his play? Maybe he was such a master at the art of seduction that he got a girl to relax by making her believe he was totally into her? "Well, here I am," she said brightly. "In all the years we've known each other, have we ever had a conversation? I don't think we have."

He shook his head sadly. "When you first came here, you dismissed me, and I've been nursing a broken heart ever since."

She laughed out loud. "You're so full of shit!"

His eyes widened. He did a good job of looking hurt. "I am not." His lips quirked up a little. "Well, maybe, sometimes, but what I just said? That's God's honest truth. When I first laid eyes on you, I thought we were going to have a beautiful friendship." He waggled his eyebrows, making her laugh again. "But you put me in my place in no uncertain terms."

She gave him a puzzled look. "Are you serious?"

He nodded solemnly. "You don't remember?"

"No."

He blew out an exaggerated sigh. "She broke my heart, and she doesn't even recall. We were all up at the big house, Uncle Cole and Aunt Madeleine's. It was the first time you'd been over there. I asked if you wanted to walk the estate with me and you turned me down."

Mary Ellen furrowed her brow as she tried to remember. It came back to her. She'd been talking to Cameron's father, who was still on the board at the time, when Antonio had asked if she wanted to go for a walk with him. She'd thought he was gorgeous even then, but it didn't seem right to go sneaking out back with a guy when she'd been invited to a gathering at her new employer's home. "I'd completely forgotten about that." She laughed. "But now you mention it, I seem to recall that when I said no, you went for your walk with Elaine from HR."

He tried to look contrite, but she could see he was hiding a smile. "I had to do something to distract me from my heartbreak. That's all I've been doing ever since."

She shook her head at him. "Don't. We both know that if I'd said yes, Elaine's turn would just have been delayed a day or two."

He hung his head. She hadn't expected him to be this playful. She'd expected him to be on a mission, to be charming or whatever was needed to ensure that she would fall into his bed at the end of the night. "If it's any consolation, I regretted saying no."

When he lifted his head, he was grinning. "You did? I believed you never gave me a second thought."

"Oh, come on. You're Antonio Di Giovanni." What else could she say? She could hardly tell him how much she'd thought about him, or the fact that it was mostly at night, in bed, by herself. She felt her cheeks flush. What would he do with that knowledge? She'd never know because he'd never find out. "Let's be real here. It's you who never gave me another thought."

"That's not true. I think about you a lot."

It was her turn to grin. "You do?"

"I do. I'm not going to go into all the details." He gave her that sexy smile again, and it hit her like a shockwave, making her belly clench. If he was just working his lines, they were having the desired effect. "I wouldn't want to embarrass either of us, but yes. I think about you."

She nodded and looked up with relief when the waiter came to take their order.

"What changed?" she asked when he was gone.

"Changed?"

"You said you think about me. I would never have guessed that. And that's not like you. You don't normally leave a woman guessing."

He shook his head. His smile was gone. Had she messed up? Was she calling him on his bullshit and he didn't like it? She hoped not, but she'd started to relax with him. He'd started to feel like a friend, and she was a straight shooter with her friends.

To her surprise, he reached across the table and took hold of her hand. She let him.

"Mary Ellen. Do you want to know the truth?"

She nodded.

"The truth is I wasn't ready for a woman like you. I'm not sure I am now, but I'd like to find out."

"What do you mean?"

"I mean … I've played the field. I've had fun. I've done all the meaningless sex. You're not like that. With you, it would be meaningful. I wasn't grown up enough before. I think I am now. I'd like to find out. Would you?"

She stared at him for a long moment, trying to puzzle out what he was talking about. If it was a line, it was a really tacky one. Did women really go for that? Sex with you will be meaningful, so on your back sweetie? Maybe they did. It didn't do anything for her, though.

He was still holding her hand, waiting for her to reply. What could she say? Yes, she wanted to sleep with him, but the friendship she'd thought they might be starting here? That was probably out the window if he was feeding her lines like that. She smiled. "I don't think it'll be meaningful, but I think it could be fun."

He squeezed her hand and let go. Sitting back in his chair, he looked so solemn. "You don't see me as someone you'd want to date?"

She laughed. "I didn't think you dated? At least, not more than once or twice."

"I don't generally."

She really wasn't sure what he was trying to do. She'd wanted to make it clear that yes, she was up for sleeping with him, but he was still trying to feed her lines about dating. "At the risk of blowing it here—cut the crap, okay?"

"That's what I'm trying to do. I'm trying to be upfront, no BS, and ask you if there's a chance of us dating—getting to know each other."

It was Mary Ellen's turn to sit back. "Seriously?"

He nodded.

"I thought you just wanted ... to ... you know."

The hint of a smile played on his lips. "Of course I want that. But more than that, I'd like for us to go out, for real. What do you think?"

Wow. That wasn't what she'd been expecting. "You and me? Date? For real?"

He nodded. "For real."

"Wow." She laughed.

Antonio wasn't laughing. He was watching her intently. "You think it's funny?"

"No. Yes. Oh, God. I don't know. It's just so unexpected."

"But you're not saying no?"

She shook her head.

He smiled. "Does that mean you're saying yes?"

"Yeah. Why not?" Who knew what had come over him that he thought he wanted to go out with her, but yeah, she was up for it. Why not?

He leaned forward and reached for her hand again. "I won't disappoint you."

She wanted to laugh but bit it back. He never had yet, but he didn't know the first thing about that.

Muse was starting to get crowded by the time they'd eaten. It was Friday night, after all. Antonio wanted this to be special. He didn't want to stay here and dance with Mary Ellen then take her home. That wouldn't be special enough. He'd done that too many times with too many women. "Do you want to get out of here?"

"Okay." The way she smiled made it plain that she thought he meant the obvious—did she want to go somewhere they could get naked. He'd love to, but that wasn't part of the plan. He was going to wait for that. That would certainly make it special—and different.

Once they were out on the street, he slung his arm around her shoulders. "Do you want to walk?" He figured they could walk down by the river; that would be romantic.

He was surprised when she smiled up at him. "Do you have your car here?"

"Yes. Why?"

She laughed. "You'll probably think this is crazy, but I've always wanted a ride in your car. I think it's awesome."

He chuckled. "Your wish is my command." If she wanted to ride in the Maserati, he'd be happy to take her. He knew exactly where they could go, too.

He opened the door for her to get in and she grinned. "Thanks. This is so cool."

He smiled back, happy that she was genuinely interested in the car that he loved so much, but a little disconcerted that she seemed more interested in it than she was in him.

The evening was still warm, and the breeze ruffled his hair as he took the road out of town. He looked over at Mary Ellen; she wasn't one of those women who asked him to put the top up. She sat there grinning with her hair blowing wildly around her face. She was amazing.

Much as he loved his convertible and usually liked the fact that it kept conversation to a minimum, he was glad when he reached the winery.

She raised an eyebrow at him as they waited for the electronic gate to open before them. "You brought me to your work?"

He laughed. "No. I brought you to the place I'm passionate about. I brought you to one of my favorite places in the world."

She smiled. "Cool. I didn't know that about you."

That surprised him. As he pulled the car forward, he wondered who she thought he was, if she didn't know that his wines were his life.

Chapter Six

Antonio parked the car in front of a beautiful house. Mary Ellen looked up at it and smiled. She'd never been here before, but she'd seen the house plenty of times on the label of the Di Giovanni wines. "It's even more beautiful in person."

Antonio smiled. "Isn't it? I love this place."

"You don't live here, do you?" Part of her wanted him to say yes, that he did live here, which meant that his bed was here, and he was taking her to it. Much as she liked that idea, she knew his house was up in the hills; she'd been there a couple of times to his famous parties.

"No, though I stay here often."

Hmm, he must have a bed here, then. Damn. She had to stop thinking about that. It'd happen soon enough, she was sure of it. For now, she should simply enjoy his company. She was starting to understand why everyone did. He wasn't just charming. He was fun and smart. He was easy company, good company. She could see him becoming a real friend. She liked the idea of dating him—whether it lasted a week or a whole month, she already knew she'd enjoy it.

He held his hand out to her. "Do you want to walk?"

The dusk was settling over the vineyards—the last of the reds and purples fading to blue and gray. "I'd love to." She wasn't going to wonder if this was a standard move—a romantic walk to get a girl in the mood. She took hold of his hand, and he led her around the side of the house and out into the vineyards beyond.

"Do you walk the vines often?" he asked.

Mary Ellen shook her head. She knew it was something Chelsea loved to do, and Cameron went out at least once a week to check the grapes and check in with the foremen and chat with the laborers.

Antonio looked puzzled, if not disappointed.

"I don't feel as though I know enough," she explained.

That just made him look even more puzzled.

"I know I work with wine, I love to drink it, I can tell you about all the processes, but out here I feel like an imposter. It's not in my veins, not like you and Cam and Chelsea. For me it's all learned from books."

Antonio smiled and held her hand tighter, leading her down a row of vines. "That's all the more reason you should come out here. Get to know the land, the vines, the grapes themselves." He stopped and cupped a handful of leaves gently to sniff them. Then he gestured for her to do the same.

She felt a little self-conscious as she leaned forward. Was he teasing her? Each grape had its own smell, she knew that much, but leaves didn't smell, did they? She was surprised to discover that they did. They smelled like springtime, and she smiled up at him. "Wow."

He nodded. "Get to know them, spend time with them, you'll learn to appreciate them, and then you won't feel like an outsider anymore. You'll feel like you belong." He smiled down at her. "And I think you do."

Oh. When he smiled like that it made her wish she did belong—with him. His face was so handsome—and so familiar, she'd pictured it so often over the last few years, but the expression on his face, the tenderness of his big brown eyes made her wonder again what it would be like if he actually cared about her.

She sucked in a deep breath as he let go of the leaves and moved his hand to cup her cheek. The feel of his fingers on her skin sent heat-waves rushing through her.

"I believe you do belong here," he murmured as he lowered his lips to hers.

She couldn't make her brain focus on what he might mean by that. All coherent thoughts fled as his arm slid around her waist, drawing her to him. He kissed even better than she'd imagined. His lips were warm and soft, his body hard. His arms felt strong around her, and that was all she was aware of as she parted her lips to kiss him back. His tongue explored her mouth, and she clung to his shoulders to keep herself upright. She'd never thought of herself as the swooning type, but his kiss made her knees buckle.

It was a long time before they came up for air, and she didn't want to even then. She could have kissed him like that all night. He lifted his head but kept his arms tight around her. "You do."

She cocked her head to one side, not understanding. "I do what?"

He raised an eyebrow, then shook his head slightly. "Kiss better than anyone I've ever known. I always thought you might."

She didn't know what to say. Had he really ever spent time wondering how she might kiss? She'd certainly wondered about him, but to think that he ...? No. She smiled. "I'll bet you say that to all the girls."

He gave her a rueful smile. "Believe what you like."

~ ~ ~

Antonio took her hand again and walked on. This was one of his very favorite places on earth. He walked out here almost every day. Some people went to church. Some people meditated. He walked the vines. Alone. He'd wanted to bring her out here, and he was glad he had. He'd brought a couple of women out here over the years but usually regretted it. Sharing this place was like sharing a piece of his soul. Women in the past had missed the point entirely. Mary Ellen didn't really get it either. But she felt right out here. She wasn't chattering away, oblivious how important this was to him, nor was she feigning some connection that she didn't feel. She'd been honest with him. She didn't feel like she belonged. He could understand that. Wine might not flow in her veins like it did with his family, but he was starting to believe that she could belong here and that he wanted her to.

The sky was almost dark now; he looked up at the first stars twinkling down on them. It felt like a sign. He slung his arm around her shoulders as they walked on, wanting to feel her closeness. The blood rushed to his pants as her full breast brushed against his chest. Resisting temptation wasn't normally his thing, but he was determined that tonight he would manage it. Mary Ellen wasn't the type to sleep with him on the first date, and not even attempting to would mark this as something new and special for him.

"How old were you when you first came here?" she asked.

"I don't really know. When we were kids, we split all our time between Sicily and here. We went to grade school over there and spent all the holidays here, then we came here for high school and went back every summer."

Mary Ellen nodded, looking thoughtful. "So, do you think of yourself as American or Sicilian?"

"Both." He smiled. "I feel like I belong wherever I am."

"That must be nice."

"You should try it. It's a good feeling. Right now, imagine that you belong right here." He tightened his arm around her shoulders. When he said right here, he meant by his side, and he, too, was imagining how that would feel. He liked it.

The look she gave him suggested that she understood what he meant, but didn't quite believe it. She looked around and then back at him. "I think it would be wonderful to belong here. I can imagine it, but ..." She shrugged. "This isn't where my life has taken me."

He wished there wasn't a but. He wanted her to be able to imagine her life being here with him. But this was their first date, after all. He had time. He loved the idea, but they were just getting started. He didn't need to push things along. "I believe life can take us wherever we want to go—if we want it enough."

She looked up at him, and he wondered again if she understood what he was really saying.

"Tell me about your life. Where did you grow up? How did you get into the wine business?"

She smiled. "I'm afraid my childhood wasn't as glamorous as yours. I grew up in suburbia in Ohio. I went to college in Oregon and got interested in wine while I was there. I worked at a small winery in the Willamette Valley. I loved it there, but ..." She shrugged. "Things went bad, and I applied for the job with Hamilton-Groves. The rest, as they say, is history."

"So, did you work with David?" Antonio wished he hadn't asked, but he never had been able to keep his questions to himself.

She nodded and stepped away from him. "Yeah, we met at work. He was one of the sales reps, and I was assistant to the CEO." She made a face. "We got engaged, then he met the CEO's daughter, and apparently, she was a better opportunity for him than I was."

Antonio slid his arm around her waist and drew her back to him. "I'm sorry. I didn't mean to upset you."

She smiled brightly, but she felt tense. "You didn't."

He slid his hand up her back and closed his fingers around the back of her neck, stroking the soft skin under her hair. "I'm sorry he hurt you, but as I told him, I'm grateful that he did." She looked up into his eyes, and he nodded. "I am. Where would you be now if you'd married him?"

She pursed her lips and shook her head.

"All I know is that you wouldn't be standing here with me." He dropped a kiss on her forehead and smiled. "I'm sorry he hurt you, but I'll be forever grateful to him." He lowered his head to hers. He needed to kiss her, to tell her how glad he was that she was here with him now. His lips brushed thin air as she pulled away with a frown.

"It's very sweet of you to say all that, but come on."

"Come on?"

"Cut the bullshit, would you? I'm not some starstruck tourist, and I'm certainly no model or actress. You don't need to dream up the perfect lines that you think a woman wants to hear. Not with me. You don't need to feed me lines to get me into bed."

Antonio stepped back. She might as well have slapped him. He'd been honest with her, and she thought he was playing her. He took a deep breath. He could see why she might believe that. "I'm sorry. I'm not feeding you lines. I know better than that—I know you wouldn't fall for them. I was telling you the truth."

She pursed her lips.

"I was. Perhaps with time, you'll come to believe me."

She blew out a sigh. "I think with very little time, we'll have bonked each other's brains out and be on our way. All I ask is that you don't feed me bullshit. I don't like it, and I don't need it."

He smiled. He couldn't help it. She wasn't going to make any of this easy for him. "I promise you. I will feed you no bullshit. Can I ask you to promise me something?"

"What?"

"Promise me you'll keep an open mind? Give me a chance? How would you feel right now if you believed everything I've told you?"

He watched her think it over. "If I honestly believed that you thought I belong here? If I believed that you were grateful to David for setting me free, so I could be with you?"

He nodded and waited.

She shook her head, but he could see the hint of a smile playing on her lips. "If I believed all of that were true, I think I'd be happy." She met his gaze and nodded. "I would; I'd be happy."

He was thrilled—there was hope.

"But I don't believe it," she added when she saw his grin.

"Not yet, but will you promise me that you'll stay open to the possibility?"

She narrowed her eyes. "You want me to stay open to your bullshit?"

He laughed. "I promise you, it's not bullshit."

"So, you're telling me that we're going to date and you're going to magically and miraculously fall in love with me?"

He drew in a deep breath. He had a sneaking suspicion he was already falling for her, but this may not be the time to admit it. Instead, he nodded. "Stay open to the possibility?"

She shook her head. "I'm sorry, but that's too ridiculous for words."

"No. It isn't. Anything's possible. You never know; you might even fall for me."

Her head shot up, and her eyes widened, a reaction that surprised him—he'd half expected her to laugh.

"Do you concede that's possible?"

She nodded slowly. "Like you said. Anything's possible."

~ ~ ~

Mary Ellen was quiet in the car on the way back. He was taking her home. He hadn't even suggested that they should go inside the house, visit the apartment that he kept there. She was kind of glad of that now. She'd felt icky when he'd said all that stuff about being grateful to David. Guys didn't talk like that, not unless they were telling a woman what they thought she wanted to hear. And the only reason they told women what they wanted to hear was in order to get on their good side, to get something they wanted—usually sex. She'd been disappointed to think that he was just using the right words to get what he wanted. She'd started to relax with him, to feel like they were friends. She stared out the window. She couldn't bring herself to believe the other possibility—the possibility that he was telling the truth. That he really was that into her, that he was glad she wasn't with David anymore, and that he truly could see her belonging at the winery—with him.

She watched the stars twinkle in the dark sky above. Was it really possible that he could somehow fall for her? She doubted it. What she didn't doubt was that, as he'd suggested, she could let herself fall for him—if she wasn't careful. She didn't need to worry. She'd taught herself to be very careful around men. She'd dealt with heartbreak once, she had no intention of having to deal with it ever again.

Antonio reached across and took hold of her hand. "Are you okay? You're very quiet over there."

"I'm fine." She smiled back at him. "How about you? Has this evening been a disappointment for you? Are you going to drop me home and then go find someone who will go for your lines?"

He gave her a rueful smile. "What happened to that open mind you were going to have?"

She laughed. "I'm struggling with that."

"Okay. How about you just give me some time, then? Let me prove to you that I'm not full of it."

She raised an eyebrow. "You want to do this again?"

"I do. Tomorrow night?"

"Okay, but don't worry if you get a better offer. I'll understand."

He brought the car to a stop in front of her apartment building and cut the engine, then turned to look at her. "I won't understand if you do."

She had to smile. If she didn't know him, she might be fooled by the dark look he gave her. She might believe that he was the jealous Italian he appeared to be. "All I had planned for tomorrow night was a bubble bath."

He smiled. "That could still be arranged."

She laughed.

"I mean, at my place. After dinner."

Mary Ellen pressed her lips together, hoping he couldn't see the effect that thought had on her.

He didn't seem to notice; he was too busy unfastening his seat belt and getting out of the car. Oh. So, he planned to come in with her now? Why not? She went to open her door, but he was there opening it for her and helping her out. She fished her keys out of her purse and let them into the lobby.

She didn't know what to say as they waited for the elevator. This wasn't a situation she'd found herself in in a very long time. She felt embarrassed and excited at the same time. She was finally going to sleep with Antonio Di Giovanni—the real-life version.

She was so nervous, she jumped when the elevator dinged. He smiled and gestured for her to enter ahead of him. They rode up in silence, and she was a little disappointed that they weren't all over each other. She'd imagined him to be the kind who'd have a girl pressed up against the wall, hot kisses, hands everywhere. He must be saving it for when they made it to her apartment—she hoped.

Her keys jingled in her hand as she unlocked the door. She pushed it open and looked up at him, not sure what to say, wishing he'd make it easy for her.

He smiled down at her and tucked his fingers under her chin, tilting her head back. This was it, here came the passionate kiss that would ignite everything. No. He planted a chaste kiss on her lips and stepped back. "I'll pick you up tomorrow ... does seven work?"

She nodded mutely, stunned that he was leaving. He lifted her hand and kissed her knuckles. "Ciao, bella."

She stood in the doorway and watched him walk back to the elevator. When he reached it, he turned around and smiled.

"You don't want to ...?" She couldn't believe she'd asked, but she couldn't help it.

He nodded solemnly. "I want to, bella. You have no idea how much I want to."

For some reason, her disappointment came out as anger. "Oh, I think I get the idea. After all, you're there." As if to reinforce her point, the elevator announced its arrival with a ding and the doors slid open. "I'm here. Goodnight."

She turned to go inside, shocked at her outburst. She doubted she would see him tomorrow after that. It turned out she didn't need to wait that long. He was back at her door before she had chance to close it. He closed his arms around her and backed her against the wall, just like she'd imagined in the elevator. He claimed her mouth in a kiss that left no room for doubt whatsoever. Even if she hadn't been convinced by that kiss, the feel of his hard-on pushing between her legs told her in no uncertain terms, that yes, he did want her. His hands roved over her, and her arms reached up around his neck, clinging on for dear life as he swept her away with a kiss she knew she'd never forget.

When he finally lifted his head, they were both breathing hard. He placed his hands on the wall on either side of her head but continued to rest the weight of his body against her. She closed her eyes and tried to calm her racing heart. All she could feel was his hot, hard cock pushing between her legs.

He smiled. "Just to be clear, I'm trying to be a gentleman here. I wasn't feeding you lines to get you into bed earlier. You can be certain of that because I made a promise to myself that I wouldn't even try to get you into bed. Not tonight." His brown eyes held an intensity she hadn't seen in them before. She felt it, too. She wanted to take him by the hand, lead him into her bedroom and explore the passion that was crackling in the air between them.

"I want you," she breathed. At this point, she had no shame. She had nothing but desire to finally be with him.

He claimed her mouth again, kissing her senseless before all too quickly lifting his head again. "I want you." He closed his hand around her breast, making a low moan escape from her lips. He rocked his hips, making her move in time with him. "You have to know how much I want you. But a promise is a promise, bella. Not tonight. Tomorrow. Will you come to me tomorrow?"

She nodded, and he cupped her face between his hands, kissing her deeply one more time. "Goodnight, Mary Ellen." He turned and left.

Once she'd closed the door, she leaned back against it. Her hands were shaking, and she was out of breath. She went through to the bedroom and looked at herself in the mirror. "Tomorrow," she told herself. Tonight, she would no doubt toss and turn for hours, wishing he'd stayed and wondering if he could possibly have meant even half of what he'd said. Part of her thought he might be playing some horrible game with her, but that was just fear and insecurity talking, and she knew it. The rest of her was half afraid, half excited about what might be happening between them.

Chapter Seven

Antonio pushed his chair back from his desk and ran his hands through his hair. He'd thought that coming into the office would help distract him, but it seemed that nothing could. It was now two-thirty on Saturday afternoon. Fourteen and a half hours since he'd somehow managed to walk away from Mary Ellen's apartment. Four and a half hours until he'd see her again—until he could make up for what he hadn't done last night. He'd thought he was doing the right thing, thought he was respecting her, being honorable. The look on her face when he'd left and the ache in his balls ever since told him that what he'd been was stupid. He could have stayed, could have spent the night with her, learning her, loving her, getting to know every inch of her body, tasting her creamy skin. He balled his fists and banged them together. He hadn't done it. He needed to stop thinking about it for the next four and a half hours. Then he would make damned sure he made up for it.

He paced his office, wondering what he was going to do to kill time between now and seven. He'd normally walk the vines, but he knew it would just remind him of her. She'd looked so beautiful in the moonlight. He should have undressed her out there, laid her down and … dammit, no! He needed to do something.

He smiled and picked up the phone. He'd call home. Check in with his parents and his brother Marcos. He hadn't talked to them yet this week—he'd been a little distracted. He decided to call Marcos first. He'd been concerned about him lately. It seemed that his breakup with his wife Caterina was finally permanent. Antonio didn't like the woman, but he still felt bad for Marcos. He wasn't used to failing at anything, and the thought of failing at marriage was what had kept him trying long after most men would have walked away.

"Pronto." Marcos picked up on the third ring.

"Pronto."

"Antonio!"

"Hey, brother. How are you?"

"I'm alive. And you?"

"I'm good. What's going on with you?"

Marcos sighed. "Misery and divorce. How about you?"

"I'm sorry."

"No, you're not. Neither am I. It's good that it's finally over. We haven't been together for nearly two years."

"You haven't? But I thought ..."

"You thought what we wanted you to think, just like everyone else. She's been fucking Lorenzo all that time. Neither of us wanted the shame of the world knowing about it."

"Damn. I'm sorry."

"There's no need. It's all worked out. I'm rid of her. I'm free."

"Well, in that case, congratulations."

"Thanks. I don't feel like celebrating yet. First, I need to learn how to start living again. I've been a bitter, angry man for too long."

Antonio was surprised by his brother's honesty. "I didn't like to mention it."

Marcos laughed. "Because you're a wise man. Now it's behind me."

"And you can get back to focusing on being happy and making great wines?"

"Being happy, at least."

"And the wines?"

"I don't know, Toni. I've lost the love."

"Wow! I never thought I'd hear you say that."

"Me neither. Maybe it's just temporary. I'll take some time, see how I feel when the divorce is final."

"Yeah, it'll come back, I'm sure. You've been under a lot of pressure from all angles. You'll be fine." He couldn't imagine his brother losing his passion for winemaking.

"Anyway, what about you? What have you been doing? Or should I ask who? Anyone I might have seen on TV lately?"

"No, tell me if this is the wrong time to talk to you about it, but I think I've met someone special."

Marcos laughed. "Don't worry, just because I'm getting divorced, I'm not going anti-women on you. I'll get it right next time. I wasn't sure you would ever think of one woman as special though. I thought they were all special to you, and there are so many of them."

Antonio chuckled. "That's the way I've always seen it, but Mary Ellen's made me change my mind."

"Mary Ellen? Cameron's Mary Ellen? His assistant?"

"The one and only."

Marcos let out a long, low whistle.

"What?" asked Antonio. "What does that mean?"

"It means I think my little brother is all grown up. Mary Ellen is the real deal. I like her, but she wouldn't stand for your shit."

Antonio laughed. "Don't I know it. I'm being more honest with her than I've been with any woman—and would you believe she thinks it's bullshit?"

Marcos laughed. "Tell me you're not going all heart on your sleeve, professing undying love?"

Antonio pursed his lips. "Not that bad, no. I just let her know that I see hope for us."

"Hmm, and she didn't like that?"

"She just doesn't trust that I mean it."

"And how long have you been seeing each other?"

"Ah."

"Ah, what?"

"Now you're going to laugh at me. I told her that last night."

"And let me guess, you've been seeing her a whole week?" Marcos chuckled.

"Actually, no. Last night was our first date."

"Antonio!"

"What? It's true. And it's not like we just met. We've known each other for years."

"Maybe, but you don't really know each other. It's not as though you've been friends. In fact, if I remember rightly, the two of you barely ever talk even when you're in the same room. You were always scared of her."

"Not scared, exactly …"

Marcos laughed. "No, maybe not, but wary at least."

"Yeah, I'll admit that much, but I'm not wary anymore. I think this might be it, Marcos."

"I hope it is. I like her, but take your time. For your sake and for hers. Get to know her first, get to be friends. It's better to fall in love with a friend than a stranger."

"Do you think you'll come back and see your friend, now that you're getting divorced?"

"It's too soon to think about that."

Antonio nodded. He knew he shouldn't bring it up, but he'd always felt Marcos made a mistake marrying Caterina. He should have married the girl he'd called a friend but had been in love with since junior year of high school. "I hope you will."

"What? Come and see you or come and see her?"

"Both, but especially her."

"Is she still single? Do you think it could ever work?"

"Yes and yes."

Marcos was quiet for a long time, and Antonio knew it was best to wait and see what he might say.

"Anyway. It's late here. I should go. Thanks for checking in."

So that was it. Marcos didn't want to talk about it. "Okay, brother. Let's talk again soon?"

"We will. Love you, little brother. Ciao."

"Love you. Ciao. Ciao." Antonio hung up and shook his head. He hoped Marcos might come back and visit, but even if he did, how could things work out differently for him than they had all those years ago? Marcos had been bound and determined to return to Sicily to run the family vineyard there. That had made it impossible for him to be with a girl who was just as determined to stay right here in Napa to run her own family's business. He'd love to see them get back together, but he didn't see how it could work out for them even now.

Marcos would figure things out. He'd have to get through his divorce and get right with himself before he could think about anything else. Antonio, on the other hand, felt as though he was on the cusp of his new life right now. He'd have to remember Marcos's caution to take things slowly, or at least to not rush Mary Ellen. He should get to know her as a friend and then maybe they could build something beautiful together, something to last a lifetime. He grinned at the thought. It didn't even surprise him. Up to this point, he'd only ever looked to share something with a woman that would last a night-time, but he'd always known that when he was ready, he'd want to settle down and give his heart to the right lady.

He was beginning to believe that Mary Ellen was that lady, but he needed to be sure of it himself before he started trying to convince her of it, too. Tonight, they would have fun, get to know each other better. He'd cook for her, they'd talk—and later, he'd take her to bed and love her till she believed him.

He closed up the office and headed for town. He needed to stop by the grocery store, and then he'd go home and cook.

~ ~ ~

Molly came and climbed up on the stool next to Chelsea. "Sorry, ladies. I thought the rush was never going to end."

"Don't worry about it, we're fine sitting here," said Chelsea. "You work too hard, though. You should hire a manager so you can take more time off."

Mary Ellen nodded her agreement. "I wish you would. You're here every night and every weekend. You don't even close on Mondays anymore. You know what they say about all work and no play."

"I've been thinking about it," said Molly. "It might be time."

Mary Ellen and Chelsea exchanged a stunned look. Then Chelsea reached across and placed her hand on Molly's forehead as if to test her temperature. "Are you feeling okay? Did you really just say that?" The two of them had been telling Molly for years that she needed to bring in a manager to share the workload. Until today, she'd always claimed she didn't need any help.

She smiled. "I'm feeling fine, but I'm finally starting to agree with the two of you. I need a life outside of this place. I want to go places, do things, have fun."

"Get a boyfriend?" suggested Chelsea.

Molly shook her head at that. "I'm not there yet. I'm not looking for someone; I'm just feeling the need to get out and live before I get old and die."

"I think you've plenty of time left before you get old," said Mary Ellen with a smile.

"But you don't need to waste any more of it working yourself into the ground in here. Let's write up an ad and start the hunt for someone now before you change your mind," said Chelsea.

Molly laughed. "I'm not going to change my mind, but I don't want to work on it right now. This is my afternoon off; I want to enjoy it, relax and have fun with you two." She looked at Mary Ellen. "I want to hear all your news—especially about what went on with Antonio the other night."

"Oh, forget the other night," said Chelsea with a grin. "That was just a catalyst for everything that's happened since. She went out with him last night, and she's seeing him again tonight."

Molly grinned at her. "You did? You are? That's awesome! You have to tell me everything." She dug Chelsea in the ribs. "And you have to be quiet and let her catch me up."

Mary Ellen laughed at the indignant look on Chelsea's face. "Don't worry, Chels. I'll be quick." She filled Molly in on everything that had happened since she'd last seen her in here on Wednesday. At least, almost everything. She finished at the part where Antonio drove her home from his winery last night.

When she finished, Molly and Chelsea looked at each other then back at her. "So, now we're to the good bit, right?" asked Molly.

Chelsea pursed her lips. "Exactly. I don't believe any evening with Antonio ever ended with a chaste kiss goodnight at the door."

Mary Ellen felt the heat in her cheeks. "Well, sorry ladies, but it did. He was trying to be a gentleman, and he didn't believe that I would sleep with him on a first date anyway."

Molly laughed. "Oh my God! What have you done to him? I always thought Antonio believed that any woman would sleep with him on a first date."

Mary Ellen rolled her eyes. "Me too. Honestly, I don't know if I'm touched that he's being honorable or pissed that he sleeps with everyone except me on the first date."

"I think it's amazing," said Chelsea. "I really do. I mean, even the fact that it's a first date. How often does he do a second date? And he wants the two of you to date, like, to see each other. You've got him all turned around."

"You really think so?" Mary Ellen was looking for reassurance. She'd tossed and turned for hours last night. He'd left her hot and horny but also confused. She wanted to believe that he was as into her as he claimed, but at the same time, she didn't dare to for fear of ending up disappointed and looking stupid.

"It sounds like it to me," said Molly. "I've always thought the two of you would make a great couple."

Mary Ellen sighed. "Me, too—at least, physically. You know how I am about him. But come on, this is Antonio we're talking about. Antonio who's with a different woman every time you see him. Antonio who plays the field. Antonio who doesn't date, who always has a beautiful, willing starlet on his arm. I just don't see him getting into a real relationship—and least of all with me."

"Everyone reaches a point where they settle down sooner or later. Just look at Cameron. He was as bad as Antonio until he met Piper."

"I wouldn't say he was that bad."

"Okay, not quite, but you know what I mean. Maybe Antonio's just reached his point where he wants more out of life, where he wants to share it with someone special and somehow what happened between the two of you in here the other night made him realize that that someone special has been right under his nose all along."

"But why would he suddenly go from no interest in me whatsoever to wanting to date?"

Chelsea made a face. "Maybe the same reason you have. Even up until Wednesday afternoon, you swore you had no interest in dating him. He wasn't someone you were interested in as a person. He was just good to look at, remember?"

"Yes, but I didn't know who he was. I had the wrong idea about him. I …"

Molly grinned. "Maybe it's the same for him? Maybe he always thought you were stand-offish and aloof? You always seem that way when he's around. You've never had a fun chat with him or anything, have you? Maybe when he heard you talking to your mom about David, he realized that you weren't what he thought you were either. He saw your soft side for the first time and liked it."

"That'd be my guess." Chelsea nodded her agreement. "Grant said Antonio's always thought you're beautiful, but he was scared of you."

Mary Ellen choked on her drink. "He was scared of me?"

Chelsea nodded happily. "Yeah, you can come across as a real battle-axe when you want to."

Molly laughed. "I wouldn't go that far, but I can see him being a bit wary of you. You usually give him a pretty cold shoulder."

"Wow." Mary Ellen nodded. "I suppose it could have come across that way."

"Yeah, we knew you were just hiding your huge crush on him under a cool exterior, but to the rest of the world—especially Antonio—it might well have looked like you despised him."

"I never thought of that."

"Well, don't worry about it now," said Chelsea. "Now you can just focus on being your warm and friendly self with him, and he'll be totally besotted."

Mary Ellen smiled at the thought. Could he really fall for her? Could she really fall for him? It was such a pleasant surprise to discover that he wasn't the superficial guy she'd thought him to be. From what the girls said, she could understand that perhaps he was now learning—and liking—that she wasn't the cool stand-offish type he'd thought her to be. Was he really looking to change his ways and have a relationship? And was she willing to change her ways and risk opening up her heart again?

Molly grinned at her. "Look at you. You've gone all Mona Lisa smile on us. I hope this works out for you."

"We'll just have to wait and see, I guess, won't we?"

"We will," said Chelsea. "I just hope that you're prepared to give him a chance. It's a risk, you know. Are you prepared to take it? Are you prepared to give it a shot?"

Molly gave her a puzzled look, but Mary Ellen knew what she meant. She'd dated a little since she'd been in Napa, but since David, she hadn't wanted to risk getting her heart broken again. If anyone could break her heart, well, that'd be Antonio. She shrugged. "No risk, no reward."

"My point exactly," said Chelsea.

Chapter Eight

Antonio parked the car outside Mary Ellen's building at ten minutes before seven. He'd waited as long as he could. Mary Ellen had suggested that she drive herself to his place since he was cooking, but he'd said he'd come to get her. It was what a man did. That and the fact that this way he knew there was no risk of her getting in her car and going home after dinner. She wouldn't be going home until he took her, and he didn't plan to do that before morning. If it were up to him, he'd keep her for all of tomorrow—the whole week ahead, for as long as she'd stay.

He braced his hands against the steering wheel and leaned his head back against the seat. Take it easy, he told himself. Slow it down. Marcos was right. He shouldn't try to rush her. He should just be himself, have fun with her and let things happen in their own time. He checked his watch. Seven minutes before seven. By the time he got up to her apartment, he'd only be five minutes early. Maybe he'd find her not quite ready? Maybe she'd ask him to finish zipping up her dress— and he could unzip it instead. No. For one thing, Mary Ellen wasn't the type to be getting ready at the last minute, and for another, he was going to try to keep his hands off her until after dinner.

He got out of the car and strode to her building. He smiled to himself in the elevator. It'd taken every ounce of his willpower to keep his hands off her in here last night. He'd been so tempted to hit the button and make it stop, to press her up against the wall, lift her skirt up around her waist and … dammit. He was doing it again. The elevator came to a stop, and he took a deep breath as he stepped out. He needed to calm down and think thoughts of cold showers. No! That made him imagine Mary Ellen in the shower, droplets of water rolling down over her full breasts, her wet nipples standing erect. He shook his head to clear those images, while at the same time promising himself he'd see her that way for real just as soon as he could.

When he reached her door, he balled his fists, digging his fingernails into his palms in an attempt to make himself focus on the here and now. Then he knocked on the door.

It took a few moments before she answered it, long enough for him to wonder if she was checking herself over in the mirror before she did.

The door swung open, and there she was. Beautiful. He let his gaze run over her. The dress was perfect, a royal blue number that crossed over in front, exposing enough cleavage to make his eyes linger there for too long before moving on to admire the way it hugged her waist and hips, showing off her perfect hour-glass figure. Eventually, he looked up to meet her gaze.

"Hi." She smiled almost warily. Had something changed?

He hoped not, and not wanting to allow any distance to develop between them, he stepped forward and wrapped her in a hug. He breathed her in as her arms came up around his shoulders. He couldn't help it. He dropped a kiss on the soft skin in the curve of her neck. "Hi," he murmured.

Her cheeks were flushed when she stepped back. "Wow. That's some hello," she said, her nervousness still lingering.

He held her gaze. "You're lucky I was so restrained. I've counted down the hours from my foolish goodbye until this hello."

A happy smile touched her lips, but she looked away. "Do you want to come in, or should we get going?"

He stepped toward her and put his hands on her shoulders. "I'd love to come in, but we'd be here all night. We should go. I promised you dinner, and everything's ready."

She looked up into his eyes, and the way her lips parted and her breathing slowed, he thought she was going to suggest they stay here. He wouldn't have argued, but she nodded briefly. "I'll get my purse." He wanted to kiss her but instead let her move away from him. This would be their first night together; he wanted it to be at his house—to start as they meant to go on.

~ ~ ~

When he brought the Maserati to a stop in front of his house, Mary Ellen managed to get out before he came around to open the door for her. She straightened her dress and smiled up at him as he took her hand. He was so gorgeous. She wanted to pinch herself. She'd had such a huge crush on him for years, but if anyone had told her even a week ago that he was such a great guy and that she'd be here having dinner with him, she would have laughed.

He led her up the stairs to the front door. The house was beautiful. It looked like a Tuscan manor house. She'd been here before, but then it had just been the setting for his lavish parties. She'd thought of the place the same way she thought of him—handsome but soulless. Now she looked at it differently. It wasn't just magazine perfect, it was warm and welcoming, just like its owner.

He opened the front door and gestured for her to enter ahead of him. She stopped inside the grand foyer, a sweeping staircase led up to the right, and a huge chandelier hung overhead.

He stood close behind her, sending shivers racing down her spine. "Welcome. Do you like it?"

"I do. It's a beautiful place."

"It is beautiful, but more importantly, it's a good home, too." He surprised her by dropping a kiss on the top of her head. She turned to look up at him and he smiled. "It's important to me that you like it. Come through, I need to check on things."

She followed him through to the kitchen. This was a part of the house she hadn't seen before. She loved it. It was warm and cozy, better equipped than most restaurant kitchens, she was sure and bigger than her whole apartment, but it felt homey.

He pulled out a stool for her to sit at the island, then disappeared into what she assumed must be the pantry. He came back with two bottles of wine. "One for us, one for the chicken," he said.

That made her laugh. "You have an alcoholic chicken?"

He laughed with her. "You could say that." He turned to the stove and poured some wine into one of the many pans before turning back and opening the second bottle. "Do you trust me?"

She cocked her head to one side, wondering what was coming.

He gave her a half smile. "I meant do you trust my choice of wine?"

"Oh. Of course, I do."

He poured two glasses and handed one to her. "I think you'll like it."

She took a sniff and looked up at him with a smile. "How did you know?"

"Know what?" He raised an eyebrow and tried to look innocent.

"That this is my favorite?"

He shrugged. "You have good taste, obviously, and it's the best we produce."

She laughed. "When you say I have good taste—are you referring to yourself?"

He grinned. "I am."

"Modest, aren't you?" She chuckled.

"No. I am many things, but modest is not one of them. I am merely logical. You've been here, what, six years? The only time I've seen you with a date has been at fundraiser dinners, guys you've drafted in for an evening. I've never known you to have a boyfriend. Now here you are with me." He gave her a smug smile and swaggered his shoulders. "We're dating, you have no time for mere mortals, but you're prepared to take a chance on me."

Mary Ellen had to laugh. "If you weren't so damned good looking and so charming, you'd never get away with it, you know."

He gave her a half smile that set butterflies swirling in her stomach. "Oh, I do know it. You'd perhaps think I was arrogant—shallow maybe?"

Mary Ellen swallowed. Did he know that was precisely how she had thought of him?

He laughed. "Don't worry. I know I give that impression. I've always thought that people are only fooled by appearances when they don't want to look beyond the obvious."

Mary Ellen pursed her lips. "I supposed that's true. I never looked beyond appearances with you."

He gave her that sexy smile again. He knew full well how good-looking he was.

"Don't look at me like that. I admit I did judge you based on your looks, but you backed it up with your behavior."

He hung his head and looked up at her from under his eyebrows. "I have no excuses."

She laughed. "And why would you need them?"

He came to her and put his hands on her shoulders. "I'm a changed man. From now on, I'm a one-woman man."

A thrill of excitement shot through her, but she got a grip. They were just playing. He didn't mean she was his woman. "Why would you want to change? It seems to me that you enjoy life more than most, even if some people don't approve of the way you live it."

He shook his head. "Enjoyed. I used to enjoy the way I lived, but I haven't been enjoying it for a while. Last Wednesday, I'd bailed on a date and taken myself out to dinner at Molly's. I was tired of my life, tired of all the meaningless." He smiled. "And just when I reached that point, there you were."

She pursed her lips. "I've been wondering—what made you talk to me that night? We've barely spoken in all the years we've known each other. I've admitted that I thought you were shallow and arrogant. Why didn't you like me all that time? And what changed your mind?"

He held her gaze and nodded. He looked quite solemn. "Okay. Honesty time. That time I asked you to go out for a walk with me?"

"When you went with Elaine instead?"

He pursed his lips. "Yeah. I thought you were the most beautiful woman I'd ever seen. But you said no, and I was young and … enthusiastic." He gave her an apologetic smile. "I was out for a good time, and you were too close to home. You worked with Cam, and you were, I don't know, serious. No, that's not it. Too smart, maybe?"

"Too smart for what?"

"For me. All I was looking for was fun and good times."

Mary Ellen tried not to look hurt. He didn't think she'd be a good time?

He sensed her discomfort. "Let me try to explain it better? The other night at Molly's, I was sitting there thinking about how all the good times I'd been having weren't so good, that they were meaningless. When I realized it was you sitting ahead of me, I almost came to talk to you, but I didn't because I knew, with you, it would never be meaningless. With you, it could only be meaningful."

She watched his face as he spoke. He wasn't feeding her lines; he was searching for the right words, trying to tell her the truth—a truth that surprised the hell out of her.

He gave her a rueful smile. "I've always known you wouldn't put up with my bullshit. You're strong and independent; you'd see through the games and not want to play them. I thought you didn't need anything or anyone. When I saw you upset over that phone call, I knew you needed something, someone. I wanted to be there for you. I wanted to be the one to make you feel better—and in that moment, I knew I was ready for it to be meaningful." He lifted her hand to his lips and kissed the back of it before turning away to tend to the stove.

She was glad to have a moment to process what he'd said.

When he turned back, he was smiling. "So, you see, it wasn't that I didn't like you before; it was just that I wasn't ready to step up and be the man who deserves you."

"Wow."

He frowned. "It's not a line …"

She held up a hand. "No. I didn't think it was. I'm just amazed. I'm amazed how differently we've read each other up to this point. I'm amazed at the way you saw me."

"The way I do see you. You're smart, you're kind, you're beautiful."

She laughed. "I don't have any self-esteem issues, but I'm hardly beautiful compared to the kind of women you usually go out with. I'm okay, and I know how to make the most of what I've got, but I'm no great beauty, and I'm not exactly svelte and sexy."

His brows came down, and he came toward her. "You are the most beautiful woman I've ever known. Who needs svelte?" He put his hands on either side of her waist. "You're the definition of sexy. You have curves. Do you know how long I've wanted to get my hands on your curves?" As he spoke, he moved his hands up, caressing her sides and allowing his thumbs to graze her breasts. You drive me insane, Mary Ellen. I can't wait to take you upstairs, to finally undress you and to learn your curves, to know your body."

Mary Ellen's eyes drifted closed as she listened to him speak. His touch burned through her dress. She wished he'd undress her right here and now. He brushed his lips over her collarbone, and she moaned. He tangled his fingers in her hair, drawing her head back and he lowered his lips to hers. All she could do was hang on as he kissed her with a passion that spread through her whole body. He stepped between her legs, and she let them fall open, eager to feel him press against her. Her wrap-over dress fell open, and she moaned as the roughness of his pants brushed her bare thighs and the bulge inside them pressed into the heat between her legs.

He lifted his head and looked down into her eyes. "We must wait."

"I don't want to," she breathed.

He cupped her cheek in his hand and planted a kiss on her lips. "Are you sure?"

She nodded and watched as he turned off the stove and then took her hand and led her back into the foyer, up the grand staircase, and into his bedroom. The furniture was ornate, the room elegant, but she barely registered her surroundings. She was too focused on the man. The man who led her to the bed and then stopped. He sat down and patted the space beside him. This was it. She took a deep breath and sat. This was no fantasy. This was reality. She was in his bedroom, on his bed, and he was about to …

His arms closed around her and she found herself crushed to his chest as he kissed her even more deeply than before. She was so lost in his kiss she had no idea how she ended up lying on the bed in her underwear, her dress lying on the floor somewhere. He too was down to his boxers, though she'd swear his lips had never left hers.

He propped himself up on one elbow and smiled as he let his gaze run over her. "Beautiful," he breathed.

As far as she was concerned, he was the beautiful one. His muscular chest was dusted with dark hair, hair that led down in a trail that disappeared inside his boxers. She reached up, unable to resist the desire to touch. She ran her fingers down his strong arm and was amazed to see his muscles tremble under her touch.

He traced her jawline with his fingers, then ran them down her neck, over her breasts and down over her belly. She tensed. If only she'd started that diet a couple of months earlier! He gave her a puzzled look. "You don't like?"

"I like what you're doing. I just wish there was a bit less of me to do it to."

He pursed his lips. "I wish there was more of you." He closed his hands around her hips, and to her horror, he dropped his head to kiss her stomach. "Beautiful," he breathed.

She tried to push his hands away, but he gave her a stern look. "I love it, Mary Ellen. Let me?"

She nodded and then gasped as he dropped his head lower and kissed her through her panties. That felt so good, but she wished the panties were gone. Her wish was his command, and he pushed them down over her hips and lowered his head again. He grasped her hips firmly and ducked his head between her legs. All she could do was lie back and enjoy the ride as he worked her with his talented tongue. He trailed it over her entrance, up and down, then circled her clit making her moan. He spread her thighs wider and held her open to dip his tongue inside.

"Oh, God, Antonio!"

He looked up at her and smiled. "Come for me."

She nodded. As if she could argue!

He lowered his head and continued his work. She balled her fists in the sheets as he brought her closer and closer to the edge. She lost it when he slid his hands underneath her to grasp her ass at the same time he thrust deep then sucked hard. She screamed as the tension that had been building inside her let loose and tore through her in wave after wave of pleasure.

When she recovered, she noticed that his boxers were gone. Aftershocks ran through her at the sight of his cock standing proud and undoubtedly ready for action. He unfastened her bra, and she loved the look on his face as he watched her breasts spill free. She tended to think of them as something of a hindrance. They were big enough to get in the way sometimes and heavy enough to make running a problem. Antonio looked as though he'd just found the promised land. He cupped them between his hands and began to lavish attention on them with his lips and tongue. It felt so good, it almost distracted her from the fact that he was rolling onto his back, taking her with him. He was sitting up against the headboard, she was straddling him, his knees came up behind her and all the while he was loving her breasts with his tongue. Her nipples felt cold and lost when he finally let them go.

They hardened as he focused his attention between her legs, touching her, lifting her, opening her up, positioning himself, and then, "Oh, God. Antonio!" she screamed as he thrust his hips and his hot, hard cock thrust deep inside her. For a moment he was still working her clit with his fingers, then his hand was gone, and there was only the rhythm of his thrusting cock between her legs, stretching her, filling her, rocking her in his time. He cupped her face between his hands and kissed her deeply, his tongue matching the movement of his cock, making her feel like he was filling her whole body. She kissed him back, sinking her fingers into his hair while she rode him hard, feeling herself close around him, gripping him tight and drawing him in deeper with every thrust.

"Mary Ellen," he breathed, dropping his hands to her hips and his mouth to her breasts. He sucked hard on her nipple, making her scream and tighten around him as their pace became frantic. Her breasts bounced as she moved with him and his fingers dug into her hips as he tensed.

"Give it to me," he gasped as he found his release and she obeyed. Her orgasm tore through her as she moved up and down the length of his throbbing shaft. Their bodies melded together as the pleasure crashed through them, binding them together as one.

Eventually, she collapsed onto his shoulder, still shuddering as he hugged her close to his chest. She tried to get up off him, but he pulled her back down onto him one more time, making her cry out as the last ripples of their orgasm moved through him and into her.

He kissed her shoulder and smiled up at her. "You're amazing."

She raised an eyebrow. "I think you can take most of the credit for that."

He shook his head. "No, it was us; we're good at it. We make a good team."

She laughed. "I can't argue with that."

"Good, because if you did, we'd have to do it again, so I can prove to you that I'm right."

"Really?"

He nodded.

"Well ... I'm not so sure. Maybe we weren't so good at it."

He rolled her onto her back and gave her a stern a look.

She shook her head. "No. I don't think we make such a good team."

He was on top of her now, spreading her legs with his knees. "I have to prove it to you?"

She nodded and then gasped as he thrust his hips and was inside her again.

"I hope you learn to believe me. I can do this all night till you do." He moved slowly this time, in long, slow, deep thrusts that started the pleasure building low in her belly immediately.

She smiled up at him. "I might take some convincing."

He laughed and thrust deep and hard. "Hang on tight, then."

She did as he said, grasping his ass as he began to thrust his hips wildly, pounding into her as she urged him on. She brought her legs up and wrapped them around his back, which sent him over the edge. "Give it to me," he cried as she began to tense around him, her inner muscles clenching him tight as they came together. Mary Ellen could hear herself gasping and moaning as his orgasm took him and exploded deep inside her, sending her mind spinning away as her body convulsed with pleasure.

"Do you believe me yet?" he asked when they both lay spent.

She gave him a lazy smile. "Maybe."

Chapter Nine

Antonio opened his eyes and smiled. Early morning sun was streaming in through the windows—a reminder that he'd brought Mary Ellen up here to his bed before it was dark, and they hadn't left it since. Dinner still sat in pans on the stove. He'd gone down about eleven o'clock to fetch wine and cheese and crackers. They'd eaten them in bed, talking and laughing and spilling crumbs and making love again. He prided himself on his performance in bed and on his ability to make sure a woman enjoyed it. It was different with Mary Ellen. It wasn't about performance, it was about sharing. It was about taking her because he had to because something about her made him need to touch her, to taste her, to be inside her.

She stirred beside him and smiled in her sleep. Her long blonde hair fanned out on the pillow around her head. He couldn't help it; he dropped a kiss on her forehead, making her open her eyes and smile, then she closed them again and drifted back off. He couldn't blame her. It was still early, and they'd worn each other out last night. He wasn't as young as he used to be, twice in a night was his max these days—until her. He snuggled in beside her, wrapping his arm around her waist and wondering if he might be able to get back to sleep for a while.

He couldn't, and a few minutes later she opened her eyes. "I think you wore me out."

He chuckled. "I think you wore me out."

"You were the one who kept proving to me how good we are together."

"Only because you kept goading me into it by saying you doubted."

She smiled. "Oh, yeah, I did, didn't I? Just for the record … there's no doubt at all. We're amazing together."

His chest buzzed with happiness hearing her say that. "We are, but I still think we can improve." Her eyes widened, but he shook his head. "All I'm saying is that if we practice hard and often if we're dedicated to it, we can get even better."

She chuckled. "Ah, okay. I don't know about you, but I'm going to need a shower, some clean clothes, and some food before I sign up for any more practice."

"Yeah. I think we both need to get our strength back first." He knew he was right about that when his cock barely stirred at the thought of getting her in the shower. There was only so much a man could do. "Do you want to take a shower while I make us some breakfast?"

She frowned.

He hoped that didn't mean she wanted to leave instead. He cupped her cheek. "Say you'll spend the day with me?"

Her expression softened. "I'd love to, but remember that part about clean clothes? I don't really want to take a shower and then get back into my dress." She leaned over and looked at where the dress lay crumpled on the floor.

He grinned. "So how about while I make us breakfast, you take a shower, then you can wear one of my T-shirts while we take you home to get changed."

"Okay."

He planted a kiss on her lips. "You know where the bathroom is. I'll find you something you can wear. Then, how do eggs and bacon sound?"

"Great, thanks."

A little while later he was serving up breakfast when she came into the kitchen, almost making him drop the frying pan he was holding. He'd given her one of his muscle shirts and a pair of boxers to wear. If he was honest, he'd been hoping the shirt would show off her breasts, but he hadn't been prepared for the full effect. She looked fantastic. The armholes were cut low enough that he could see her bra and the vee cut in the front only served to emphasize her ample cleavage. The shirt was way too big on her, but he caught a peek of her panties underneath, and that was enough to revive him even before he'd eaten.

She smiled. "It does look good, doesn't it?"

He nodded and set the pan down. "Forgive me while I reel my tongue back in?"

"Ha. Is this your standard shirt to give the girl in the morning?"

His smile faded. He hated that she continued to think of him that way. "No. You're the first woman I've ever loaned my clothes to."

She raised an eyebrow.

"It's true. My standard is to hustle them out of here just as fast as I can. If you don't believe me, just ask Grant about the eight o'clock phone call."

"The eight o'clock phone call?"

"Yeah. It's what guys do. We have plans with our buddies that mean we're really sorry, but we have to leave by eight o'clock the morning after. The buddy gives us a call to rescue us if we're not out by eight."

To his relief, she laughed. "That's terrible."

He shrugged. "It's the way it is, but it's not the way things are with you. I need you to know this is different. You and me."

She smiled and came toward him. "I'd like to believe that."

He planted a kiss on her forehead. "Then believe it. It's true." He smiled. "If you'd like, I can start proving it to you all over again."

She laughed. "I thought we were going to eat first?"

~ ~ ~

Mary Ellen turned to look at him when he pulled up outside her building. "I told you I should have put the dress back on." She'd known it was crazy to come out in just his shirt and her panties. She couldn't run from his car to the elevator and hope no one saw her. But he'd been so persuasive, so appreciative of the way she looked—and she had to admit, she did feel kind of sexy like this. But it was different waltzing around his big house. What would happen if anyone saw her? She tried to ignore his sexy grin. "What will the neighbors think?"

He laughed. "What do you care?"

"I care that I'll have to face them again and they'll think I'm crazy."

He shook his head. "They won't think you're crazy. They'll know what you've been up to, and I'll be with you. Are you ashamed to be seen with me?"

She stared at him. She hadn't thought about that. What would the neighbors think? Would they think she'd fallen prey to the notorious Antonio Di Giovanni? She was pretty sure everyone in this town knew who he was. "I'm not ashamed to be seen with you. I just don't like the idea of them thinking I just joined the long list of your conquests."

His face darkened.

"What? Don't look like that, I was only joking with you. We both know it's true."

He shook his head. "I guess we do. It backfired on me though. I thought it was a good way to let you know that I want people to know we're together. That I don't care who sees what we're up to."

"Oh!" Wow. She hadn't thought of it that way around at all. It was true. Word of who he went out with got around, but you never heard any tales of him with a woman the next morning—and from what he'd said earlier, there was a good reason for that. He was trying to do something nice for her. In his own weird way, he was trying to tell the world they were together. She smiled. "In that case, I shall wear your T-shirt and my panties with pride." She got out of the car feeling strangely confident. Whatever people might think didn't matter much. What mattered was that Antonio was trying to make a point to her. She wasn't about to throw it back in his face.

She let them into the foyer and waited for the elevator to come down. She looked up at him and grinned. "Who knows, I might start a new trend."

He chuckled. "I doubt it somehow, no one else could pull off the look like you do."

The elevator arrived, and when the doors opened, Mrs. Jensen from the seventh floor stepped out and did a double take as she looked first at Mary Ellen, then Antonio. She recovered quickly and smiled at them both. "Good morning."

"Good morning," said Mary Ellen.

Antonio nodded and smiled politely as she passed. After a few steps, the older lady turned around and smiled back at them. "It's a great day for it," she said.

The elevator doors slid shut, and Mary Ellen burst out laughing. "She's a hoot!"

Antonio laughed with her. "And she'll no doubt have a hoot telling her tale at the bridge club."

"She plays bridge?"

He nodded. "Yeah, with Aunt Madeleine."

"Oh, my God!"

He laughed. "Don't worry about it. Aunt Madeleine and Uncle Cole will know we're seeing each other long before Mrs. Jensen gets chance to tell them."

"They will? How?"

He shrugged. "News seems to travel fast around here. Why, do you have a problem with them knowing?"

She shook her head. She didn't have any problem with it all. "I don't, but I thought you might."

The elevator reached her floor, and they stepped out. "Why would I have a problem? I want the whole world to know."

She smiled to herself as she unlocked her front door. Was this really the same Antonio? It was hard to believe he was so different—and apparently so into her.

~ ~ ~

Mondays were always crazy at the Di Giovanni winery. He wasn't sure why it was that way, but it always seemed to work out that problems cropped up, big orders came in, and surprises landed on his lap on a Monday. Today was no different. It was crazy, but he was handling it better than usual. Usually, he went into a frenzy trying to sort everything out as quickly and efficiently as possible. Today he plodded his way through one issue at a time. It felt like nothing could touch him, nothing could irritate him—he was too busy thinking about Mary Ellen. He kept smiling for no reason and chuckling about little things she'd said or done over the course of Saturday night and their day together yesterday.

"Are you okay?" His assistant Daniel had popped his head around the office door.

"I'm great, why?"

Daniel came inside looking puzzled. "Because normally by this time on a Monday you're pulling your hair out and so is everyone else. Things are normally whipped up to a frenzy by now."

"And you don't like the new calmer me?"

Daniel scowled at him. "Like? Of course, I like it. How many times a day do I tell you to calm down, to have patience? I like it, but I don't trust it. That's why I'm asking if you're okay. Is this the calm before a storm?"

Antonio laughed. "Daniel, Daniel, Daniel. I'm sorry. You're not up to speed. What you don't know is that I am a changed man."

Daniel eyed him suspiciously. "Really? And what changed you?"

"A woman. A wonderful, beautiful woman."

Daniel laughed out loud.

"I'm serious."

"Yeah, right. Unless you're talking about your mom—or wait, no, has your grandma come to visit?"

Antonio laughed. "It may seem hard to believe, but I'm serious. I met someone. She's gotten to me."

Daniel looked incredulous. "Forgive me, but won't she be gone within a week—tops?"

Antonio shook his head. "Nope. She's not a tourist or a passing fling ..."

"Or an actress or a model?"

Antonio shook his head again. "Nope. She is one of our own. A Napa girl, a wine girl, she's already part of my world, and if I get my way she's going to become a much bigger part of it."

"Who are you talking about and what are you saying?

"I'm saying she's special, and I have high hopes for us."

"Who?"

"Mary Ellen."

Daniel took a step back. "Mary Ellen? You mean Mary Ellen Greene from Hamilton-Groves?"

Antonio nodded happily.

"Holy shit! Never in a million years would I have put the two of you together."

Antonio frowned. "And why not?"

Daniel laughed. "Sorry, boss, but she's ... well, she's Mary Ellen. She's awesome, she's fun, she's a great girl, but everyone knows you don't mess with her. And you? Well, let's face it, you mess with everyone."

"Mess with?"

"You don't take things seriously. You're all about having fun. She's fun but damn, you just don't mess with her. She's like Wonder Woman or something. She organizes life into submission. I don't see you submitting."

Antonio had to stop himself from picturing her in a Wonder Woman outfit—and steer his thoughts well away from submission. He shook his head to clear it. "She's good at what she does, whatever she does." He smiled, thinking it better not to state the obvious—that she was currently doing him. "We're a good match."

"In that case, I'm happy for you both. And I'm glad she's a calming influence on you."

"She's good for me. I already know it. In fact, I think I should send her some flowers to thank her for making my day better." He picked up his phone, then looked at Daniel. "Did you need anything else?"

Daniel shook his head in disbelief. "No. I'll take care of it myself. I'll leave you to ordering your flowers."

"Great. Thanks."

~ ~ ~

Mary Ellen looked up at the sound of a knock on her office door. "Come in," she called.

The door opened, and Zoe from the reception desk stood there holding a huge bunch of flowers. "These came for you," she said with a big grin.

"Oh!" Mary Ellen felt her cheeks flush. In all the years she'd worked here, she'd never had flowers delivered to her before.

"There's a card." Zoe was still grinning.

"Thanks." Mary Ellen didn't know what else to say as she looked at the beautiful blooms. They could only be from one person, but she wouldn't have had him down as the flower sending type.

"Are you going to read the card?"

Mary Ellen smiled through pursed lips. "Not yet. I know who they're from. Don't be so nosey, anyway."

Zoe gave her a guilty smile. "I can't help it! We all know who they're from. I'm just dying to know what it says."

Mary Ellen stared at her. We all know—what was that supposed to mean? What did they know and who knew?

Zoe shrugged. "There were sparks flying between you and the delicious Antonio on Friday night, then Natasha told everyone about him following you into the bathroom. And those?" she eyed the flowers. "They aren't exactly a regular bunch of flowers, are they? They must have set him back a few hundred."

Mary Ellen looked at the flowers again. She didn't know much about them, but even she could tell they were expensive.

"Everyone's totally jealous," continued Zoe. "Who wouldn't want to go out with Antonio? Though I didn't think you'd ever fall for his charms."

Mary Ellen drew in a sigh. She liked Zoe, but she didn't want to say anything because she didn't want her personal business to become the subject of office gossip any more than it already was.

Cameron appeared in the doorway and saved her. "Hey, Mary Ellen. Do you have a minute?"

"Sure. Come on in."

"Sorry." Zoe smiled at him. "I'll get out of the way. I was just delivering these."

Cameron nodded and waited until she'd gone before he grinned at Mary Ellen. "Before you say anything, my cousin doesn't send flowers in the same way I used to."

Mary Ellen gave him a hard stare. "Who says they're from your cousin?"

Cameron laughed. "I do. The whole office probably does by now. Are you denying it?"

Mary Ellen made a face. "I don't know. I haven't opened the card yet."

"Go on, then." He plucked the little envelope out and handed it to her.

"What if I want to read it in private?"

Cam smirked. "If you insist, I'll leave, but I'll be back in two minutes, so you might as well just do it."

She opened the envelope.

Mary Ellen

This weekend was amazing. Will you spend next weekend with me too?

Want to make plans over dinner this evening?

With love,

Antonio

She couldn't help smiling as she tucked the card back inside the envelope.

Cameron had pulled up the chair on the other side of her desk. "Well?"

"Well, what?"

He gave her a sheepish grin. "Sorry. It's none of my business, is it?"

"No, it damned well isn't, you horrible man."

Cam laughed. "You know you don't mean that."

She shrugged. "No, I don't. I'm just a little bit embarrassed."

"Why?"

"Because this is all so weird. I mean, he's your cousin, for one thing. And besides, he's Antonio. Part of me feels like I'm being foolish, and everyone knows it."

"Foolish how?"

"Come on, Cam. He's notorious for going home with a different girl every night. I've just become the latest in a long line of them, and everyone knows about it."

"This isn't just about spending a night with him though, is it?"

She shook her head, wondering how much she should tell him—about what Antonio had said or about how she felt.

He was looking at her intently.

"What?"

"I know it isn't any of my business, but it kind of is, too. I care about you. I know Antonio better than anyone. I can tell you now that he doesn't see you as his latest conquest."

She nodded.

"But I think you already knew that, didn't you?"

She nodded again. "Cam, he's been up front that he wants this to be a real relationship, not just a quick fling. He's been so sweet. Actually, he's surprised the hell out of me. He's not the person I thought he was, but part of me is still waiting for him to turn around and say thanks and goodbye."

"I can understand that." He held up a hand. "I don't think it'll happen, but given his track record and your wariness of getting involved with anyone, I can see why you'd be cautious."

Mary Ellen nodded and looked at the flowers. They must have cost a fortune, but then that wouldn't matter much to Antonio.

"You like him, don't you?"

"That's hardly a secret is it?"

Cam chuckled. "Not that you like his appearance, no. You've gone gaga over his looks for years, but now you're starting to see he's a good guy, too."

She blew out a sigh. "I am." She shook her head. "It was so much easier when I thought he was an asshole."

Cameron laughed. "What's the problem? I thought you'd be happy that not only is he good-looking but he's an amazing guy, too."

"The problem, my dear Cameron, is that …" She shook her head. What was the problem? Why wasn't she absolutely thrilled that not only was her fantasy guy turning out to be a great guy but that he was also totally into her? She met Cam's gaze. "The problem is that there is no problem. There's nothing to stand in the way of him and me seeing each other, getting to know each other, dating, having a relationship. And that scares me shitless."

Cam frowned. "Why?"

"Because I'm a coward. I haven't dated anyone since David."

"I know, but I thought that was just because you hadn't met anyone you really liked."

"I made sure I didn't meet anyone so that I didn't have to take any risks. David taught me how much love can hurt. I haven't been interested in giving it another shot."

Cam smiled. "You're not a coward, you're just a realist. You don't like to take gambles. You don't want to risk getting hurt if the potential reward isn't big enough."

Mary Ellen stared at him.

"I can see you and Antonio ending up together. I think the potential reward could be huge. Don't you?"

She thought about it for a few moments. She and Antonio ending up together? Wouldn't that be something? She hadn't allowed herself to think about ending up with anyone since David. "I think it's a bit early to start talking like that."

Cameron smiled. "Maybe. Then again, maybe not."

She shook her head at him. "Anyway, what did you want?"

He chuckled. "Nothing, other than to see your reaction to the flowers."

"You horrible man." She smiled as she looked at the flowers. "I'm pleasantly surprised. Even though I don't generally subscribe to the idea of spending gobs of money on pretty things that have been cut and are going to die within a week."

Cameron laughed. "See, I told you, you're a realist. Antonio's making a big romantic gesture, and you're thinking about the practicalities. Maybe you two won't be such a good match after all."

Mary Ellen's heart sank, and a ball of disappointment settled in her stomach.

Cameron met her gaze. "No. I didn't mean that at all. I was just curious what your reaction might be when I said it. Now we both have a better idea of how you feel." He gave her a smug smile. "You're not fooling me, and I suggest you don't try fooling yourself. Why don't you give him a call to thank him for them and then meet me in the conference room? We need to start working on Q3 projections."

Chapter Ten

Antonio checked his watch. He should have left the office ten minutes ago. He just needed to wrap up the report, then he could hand it over to Daniel.

"Are you still here?"

He blew out a sigh when Daniel stuck his head around the door. "I'm almost finished."

"Why don't you go and let me work on it now. You can finish up your conclusions tomorrow. I don't need them to work on the rest."

Antonio smiled. "Yeah, I think I will, thanks."

Daniel smiled. "I'd hate for you to be late and upset Mary Ellen. I have a vested interest in her sticking around. You've been so laid back this week, she's making my life much easier."

Antonio made a face. "I'm not seeing her tonight. She's out with the girls, so I'm meeting up with Cam and Grant."

Daniel smirked. "I never thought I'd see the day. You're meeting up with the guys because she has other plans?"

Antonio tried to look stern, but he couldn't pull it off. He chuckled. "Crazy, isn't it? I've seen her every night this week, and I wanted to see her again tonight, but she already had plans with Chelsea and Piper. I tried to get her to bring them to Muse, but they're eating at Molly's."

Daniel shook his head. "It'll do you good. Keep things fresh. If you see each other every night, the flame might just burn itself out."

Antonio couldn't help smiling. "In our case, the flame keeps getting hotter and hotter."

Daniel raised an eyebrow. "You don't think it's going to burn itself out?"

"I don't." He managed to stop himself from voicing the thought about an eternal flame that came to mind. It sounded crazy enough to him, he could imagine what Daniel would think. He shut down his computer. "I just emailed you everything I've got so far. I'll get on the rest in the morning. I might not be seeing Mary Ellen, but I don't want to make Cam and Grant mad by being too late."

"They won't get mad; they're used to it."

Antonio nodded. They were. He wasn't known for his punctuality, but he was working on that. It had never mattered before, but now he wanted to be known as a reliable kind of guy—the kind who Mary Ellen could take seriously.

"See you tomorrow."

When he reached Muse, Rodney greeted him with a smile. "Your guests have arrived. I've seated them at your table. Though I will confess, I was a little surprised to see them."

Antonio smiled. "If it were up to me, I'd be having dinner with Mary Ellen, but she's out with the girls."

Rodney nodded. "It might do you good."

Antonio scowled. Why did Rodney and Daniel think he needed to cool it with Mary Ellen? He wished he could spend every minute with her. "With Mary Ellen, her presence makes my heart grow fonder. I don't want her absence."

Rodney raised an eyebrow. "I simply meant that an evening in the company of Cameron and Grant might do you good. Considering the recent developments in both of their lives."

Antonio stared at him for a moment, but Rodney simply smiled. "Would you like me to walk you to your table?"

Antonio chuckled. "No. I might be acting clueless at the moment, but I think I can still find my way out there."

"Very well." Rodney gave him one of his enigmatic smiles and turned to greet a couple who were just arriving.

Antonio bit the inside of his lip as he made his way out to the terrace. Was Rodney right? Should he be seeking advice from Cam and Grant—since they were both engaged now? He sucked in a deep breath. Was that what he was aiming for with Mary Ellen? It might be a crazy thought, considering they'd only been seeing each other for a week but was it really so crazy? He knew her, she knew him. They still had a lot to learn about each other—and about how they got along together, but so far, everything he learned about her made him fall for her more, and it seemed she was finding the same with him. She was still wary, but she was relaxing with him, and she seemed more into him every day. To say she was falling for him might be a little premature—but a guy could hope.

Cam looked up as he approached the table. "There you are. To what do we owe the honor? Ten minutes late is as good as early by your standards."

Antonio rolled his eyes. "What can I say? I'm working on being punctual."

Grant grinned at him as he sat down. "Let me guess, Mary Ellen's whipping you into shape already?"

"No." He closed his eyes, trying not to picture her with a whip, dressed in leather and fishnets and …

"Are you okay?" Cam gave him a puzzled look.

He grinned. "Yeah, sorry. I seem to get lost in my head at the mere mention of her name these days."

"Are you shitting us … or not?" asked Grant. "I can't figure this out. You seem totally besotted, and that's so out of character for you that I'm struggling to buy it."

Cameron chuckled. "That's pretty much what Mary Ellen said."

Antonio swung around to look at him. "She did? Why? When?"

"Calm down. That was on Monday when you sent her the flowers. I was prying because you're both acting so out of character I wanted to know what the deal was."

"And what is the deal?"

Cam shrugged. "I was only joking. I don't know any more than you do."

"But you said she's struggling to buy it, like him." He nodded at Grant.

"She didn't say that in so many words." Cameron was starting to look uncomfortable. "It's not my place to say anything. But if you think about it, it's hard for everyone to believe the transformation you've undergone in the last week."

Antonio nodded. He could see that. It felt completely natural to him that he should leave behind the life he'd been living and start something new with Mary Ellen, but then he knew how bored he'd been getting with his old life. No one else knew how empty it had all started to feel. "I suppose."

Grant nodded. "And from what Chelsea's said, it must be even harder for Mary Ellen to believe than anyone else."

"Why? What did Chelsea say?"

Grant shrugged. "Just about that David guy. He was supposedly Mr. Dependable, and he dumped her and humiliated her out of the blue. She's going to be wary of anyone after that, and sorry to say it, bro, but she'd have to be doubly wary of someone like you."

Antonio didn't bother to ask what he meant by that. He knew what he was, or at least who he'd been. He could never be called Mr. Dependable. He was more love 'em and leave 'em, Mr. Good Time—for a short time. He blew out a sigh and looked at Cameron.

"Don't look like that." Cameron smiled at him. "She's totally into you, you're just going to have to earn her trust, it's going to take time."

Antonio threw his hands in the air in irritation. "I don't want it to take time. I want her to know, I want to show her, to prove to her that I'm for real, that we're for real."

The others looked at him in stunned silence.

"So, you're serious about her, then?" asked Grant with a chuckle.

Antonio gave him a rueful smile. "Yeah. More serious than I've ever been about anything in my life."

"Take it slowly, then." Cameron looked serious. "You can throw your hands in the air all you like, and you can go all passionate and impatient Italian on us, but if you're that serious, you're going to have to consider what works for Mary Ellen, not just what works for you."

Antonio stared at him for a long moment. The way he saw it, he could propose to her this weekend. That was what he wanted, and surely that would convince her that he was serious. But Cameron was probably right. She would probably be more comfortable with a more conventional approach. They'd date for a while. Meet each other's families, get engaged, plan a wedding. He shook his head. He still liked his idea better.

The server came to take their order and saved him from explaining what he was thinking. He knew Cam would try to talk him down and Grant wouldn't approve either.

~ ~ ~

"Hey, ladies. I'm sorry I'm so late." Piper slid into the booth to sit beside Chelsea. "How are we?"

"Doing great, thanks. How about you?" asked Mary Ellen.

"I'm okay. It's been a long week."

"I'll bet," said Mary Ellen. "I don't envy you having to fly the sales guys around. I mean, Connor and Lyle are fun, but they're exhausting after a while."

"And we all know Cam gets jealous about it," said Chelsea with a smile.

"Aww." Piper looked so happy. "I still find it hard to believe that he gets jealous. I mean, I don't have a jealous bone in my body, but you'd think if either of us was going to get that way, it'd be me. I'm so lucky."

Chelsea rolled her eyes. "I hope when the two of you get married, you'll finally get over that. He's just as lucky as you are. You each found your perfect match." She grinned. "Just like Grant and I have found ours."

Mary Ellen nodded. She was so happy for her friends.

Piper turned to her. "And is it true about you and Antonio?"

"Is what true?" Mary Ellen stalled for time. She wanted to know what Piper meant.

Chelsea laughed. "Everyone knows you've seen each other every night this week. We've all heard the rumors about him parading you around town in your underwear. What Piper and the rest of us want to know is—is it for real?"

Mary Ellen shrugged. "I wasn't exactly parading around town, I just—"

"Nice try," said Chelsea. "You know what I mean. I wasn't asking if the rumor was for real. I was asking if the two of you are for real. It sounds like the perfect whirlwind romance."

Mary Ellen smiled. She couldn't help it. "Honestly? It feels like the perfect whirlwind romance." She sighed. "But how can it be? He's the way he is—he might whirl his way onto someone else next week. And I'm the way I am. I'm still a practical, down-to-earth midwestern girl at heart. I'm not one to be swept off my feet in a whirlwind."

"I don't see why not if it's what you want," said Piper.

"Damn, I thought you'd be the one to back me up."

Piper gave her an apologetic smile. "Sorry, but I'm living a happy whirlwind of my own."

Chelsea grinned. "You already know I'm not going to back you up. I say be brave, let that practical heart of yours ride the whirlwind and see where you land."

Mary Ellen made a face. "I'd love to but knowing my luck, I'll land right on my ass in a world of hurt."

Piper shook her head. "I don't see that happening."

"What do you know? You haven't even been here this week."

She laughed. "Perhaps not, but I've talked to Cam every night, and I've been getting blow-by-blow accounts about it."

Mary Ellen had to smile. She loved that they cared about her, even if they were less cautious about her and Antonio than she was. "Anyway. I thought this was a girl's night. We're not here to talk about men."

"No," said Chelsea. "We're here to talk about what's going on in each other's lives. I'm busy at work, happy with my man and all's well. Piper's had a tough week flying people around, but is still happily besotted with my brother, even if she is dreading the big wedding, which is looming."

Mary Ellen shot a look at Piper who nodded. "It's all good, just a bit daunting. I can't wait for us to be married, but the wedding's so big and ..." She shuddered.

"I've told her she should back it off. It's not like Cam cares. He's just doing what he thinks is right because he thinks you," Chelsea looked at Piper, "are good with it."

Piper sighed. "And I am. I'm just a little nervous. That's all, and I really don't want to talk about it. I want to forget about it tonight."

"See?" Chelsea turned to Mary Ellen. "We've covered what's going on in our lives. All that's left is to talk about what's going on in yours, and that happens to be the one and only Antonio Di Giovanni." She smiled sweetly. "So where does it go from here?"

"Can't we just date and see where it goes? Why does it have to go anywhere?"

"Because he's besotted with you, and because you've pined for him for years, and because you make such a great couple. That's why."

Mary Ellen chuckled. There was no arguing with Chelsea sometimes. "Okay. Well, as for where we're going; this weekend we're going away."

"Ooh. Where's he taking you?"

"I don't know. It's a surprise."

"That's so romantic." Piper smiled at her. "I have to tell you, I have high hopes for the two of you."

Molly came to check on their drinks. "What are we talking about?"

Mary Ellen rolled her eyes. "They're interrogating me about Antonio."

Molly smiled. "Are you enjoying yourself?"

She nodded. "I am. He's a good guy."

"He is." Molly's smiled faded. "If the two of you are going to get serious, you should maybe pin him down about where he plans to live."

Mary Ellen gave her a puzzled look. "What do you mean?"

Chelsea jumped in before Molly had chance to answer. "I don't think he ever plans to go back to Sicily."

Molly nodded. "I just think you should know what his plans are." She turned around and went back into the kitchen.

"What was that all about?" asked Piper.

Chelsea shrugged. "She has her reasons."

"What reasons?" Mary Ellen was intrigued. It wasn't like Molly to be short.

Chelsea shrugged. "Not my place to say."

"Fair enough." She couldn't argue with that, but she decided she'd pull Molly aside soon and ask her just what she'd meant. Molly might have her own reasons for bringing it up, but she'd planted a doubt in Mary Ellen's mind. She'd had a great time with Antonio this last week. She was starting to believe that the two of them might have a good thing going, but she was still wary. She didn't want to let herself fall for the guy if there was any possibility of him upping and going back to Sicily.

Piper was watching her. "I hope you're not looking for excuses to stop seeing him. He's hardly likely to just leave everything he's built here, is he? He runs the family winery."

Mary Ellen nodded. "I know; I'm just wary still. I've been dumped out of the blue once before. I don't want to set myself up for it to happen again."

Chelsea smiled at her. "I don't see that happening. I know Antonio's history doesn't make him look like a good bet for anything long-term, but he's nothing if not loyal. He's never made a commitment to a woman because when he does make a commitment, it's important to him. It looks to me like he wants to make one with you."

Mary Ellen blew out a sigh. "It does look that way, doesn't it? And if I'm honest, I love the idea, but for one thing, it's all a bit premature. We've only been seeing each other a week, and for another thing, I have trouble trusting, even with a man who makes a commitment. I've seen how easily they can be broken."

Chelsea shook her head. "You can't compare Antonio to David. That's not fair. That's like saying you're not going to drink wine anymore because you had one bad bottle."

Mary Ellen and Piper laughed at that. "Why does everything have to come back to wine around here?" asked Piper.

Chelsea laughed. "Because it's what we're all about. It's what our lives are based on."

Mary Ellen nodded her agreement. "It is, and I know you have a point. I need to judge Antonio on the way he treats me—not on the way someone else treated me in the past."

"And by the sounds of it, he's treating you very well. I can't wait to hear where he takes you this weekend." Piper looked as though she might already know.

Mary Ellen raised an eyebrow. "Are you in on it?"

Piper smiled sweetly. "It wouldn't be fair to say, either way."

Chelsea spun around to look at her. "That sounds like you are."

Piper simply shrugged. "I just hope you have a great time, wherever you go."

"Me too." Mary Ellen was looking forward to spending the whole weekend with him. If he'd gotten his way, they would have left this evening, but she'd already made plans with the girls, and no way was she going to break them. She'd already spent every evening with him this week. It had been great. He was fun and sweet, and they could talk about anything and everything. He made her laugh, and she knew he was enjoying her company, too, and not just in bed, though they had spent a fair amount of time there.

"What are your plans for the weekend?" Chelsea asked Piper.

"Nothing much. I've been away so much that we just want some quiet downtime together. And I know Cam wants me to look over some of the wedding stuff."

"You know you should just tell him if it's all too much for you," said Chelsea.

Piper shrugged. "It's fine. I know your mom and dad are looking forward to it all, and it's important to him and to them." She shrugged. "It's not like I have anyone to think about. There's just me. The only person I consider family is Laura, and she's already part of your family, so ..." She shrugged again "It's all good."

Mary Ellen couldn't imagine how that must feel. She might not be close with her folks, but she couldn't imagine them not being around. When she'd planned to marry David, the guest list had been evenly split between her people and his.

"What about you, anyway?" Piper asked Chelsea. "How long do you and Grant plan to wait before you get married?"

Mary Ellen looked at her curiously. She'd asked Chelsea a couple of times about her wedding plans, but she'd always shrugged it off.

She smiled. "We thought we'd wait until you and Cam get yours out of the way first. We'll do something much smaller and quieter. I like the idea of a beach wedding somewhere, just close family and friends. Grant likes the idea, too. Maybe in December when things are quiet." She grinned at Mary Ellen. So that should leave things clear for you for a spring or summer wedding."

Mary Ellen laughed. "Don't get too carried away. All this talk about where things are going is all well and good, but there's a long way to go between here and wedding bells."

Piper laughed. "You're right. It's fun to tease you, but just see how it goes."

Chelsea laughed, too. "I'm not teasing. I'm deadly serious. I'm making my prediction now for a summer wedding for you two."

Mary Ellen shook her head and tried to hide her smile. She and Antonio married? Part of her wanted to do a happy dance at the thought. Her more practical side wanted to put a stop to the conversation—it was ridiculous!

Chapter Eleven

Antonio smiled as he took his coffee out onto the terrace. He loved to start his days out here. He'd enjoyed it even more last week when Mary Ellen had sat out here with him. He could picture her now, sitting in her robe, sipping her coffee, and taking in the beautiful view of the valley in the early morning light. He could get used to that. He hoped he would get used to it. Last night was the first night he'd slept alone since she came here last Saturday night—and he hadn't cared for it. He'd grown too used to sleeping beside her, to waking up to find her by his side. He'd be happy for that to become his new normal—his new life. He thought back to Cameron's cautioning words last night—that he should take things at a pace she was comfortable with. He nodded reluctantly to himself. He knew that was the right way to go. He just hoped he could contain himself. She was practical; he was impetuous. It made them a good match, but he didn't want it to scare her off.

He checked his watch. It was too early to go and collect her. He'd suggested that he should pick her up from Molly's last night, so she could stay here with him, but she'd refused. She'd said it was to give her a chance to pack her things for their trip, but he had a sneaking suspicion that she hadn't wanted the girls to see him coming to get her. He could take it badly if he thought she was ashamed of him, but he knew better than that. It was more likely that she didn't want it to seem like just a booty call after they'd both been out with their friends. He smiled. She meant so much more to him than that, but he knew his reputation went before him, so he'd agreed that he'd pick her up bright and early this morning instead. Impatient, he looked at his watch again. It was only six thirty, which meant he had an hour to kill before she'd be ready. It amused him that he didn't seem to have any difficulty being punctual when it came to her.

Fifty minutes later he knocked on her door. It took a few minutes before she answered, and when she did, she took his breath away. She was dressed simply, in cut-off jeans and a white shirt, but she looked amazing. He stepped toward her and took her face between his hands. "Good morning, bella. I missed you." He planted a kiss on her lips. He'd intended it to be just a peck, but her hands came up to his shoulders, and somehow his arms found their way around her waist, pulling her against him. The feel of her full breasts against his chest made him moan. His tongue found its way inside her mouth and he was kissing her deeply before he knew what was happening. She didn't mind. She relaxed against him and kissed him back. He loved the way she kissed him. It wasn't surrender—she wasn't his to plunder—yet it wasn't a duel, either. She kissed him as an equal, something he wasn't used to. She'd let him in, then take control herself, then give it back. Her fingers tangled in his hair and she moved his head to better suit her. She was amazing.

When they came up for air, he smiled. "You didn't miss me, then?"

She chuckled. "Not much, no. Can't you tell?"

He laughed. "Not at all."

"Just give me a minute? I'm almost ready."

She disappeared into the bedroom, and he was tempted to follow her. They hadn't made love in her bed yet, and after that kiss, he'd be happy to christen it before they left. If it were up to him, they wouldn't get many chances to—she'd be living with him before long.

He went and leaned in the doorway and admired her ass as she bent down to pick up her bag. "Is that an invitation?"

She straightened up and turned around. "It could be, if you want it to, but I thought we needed to get on the road early."

He let his gaze travel over her, torn between the need to take her now and the want to make the most of their time away. He shook his head and stepped toward her. "Kiss me?"

She came to him and slid her arms up around his neck. The feel of her against him made the decision clear. He closed his hands around her ass as his mouth came down on hers. It seemed it was an easy choice for her, too. Instead of finding their way into his hair, her fingers started unbuttoning his shirt. He kneaded her gorgeous round ass and held her against his already aching cock, making her moan into his mouth. He wanted to take his time, fill his hands with her ass, her breasts, explore her with his fingers and his tongue, but there was an urgency between them this time. She had his shirt undone and ran her hands down his chest, over his abs and unfastened his jeans. He drew in a deep breath as her hand closed around him. As she began to stroke the length of him, he knew he was behind. She was still fully dressed, but he couldn't focus on anything except the feel of her hot fingers wrapped around him. She started to pump up and down in a rhythm that he wouldn't be able to take for long. He let himself enjoy a few moments, then reluctantly pulled out of her reach. He dropped his head to mouth her nipple though her shirt while he undid her jeans and pushed them and her panties down over her hips. The needy little gasps she was making stopped him from undressing her any further. They'd have plenty of time for the rest of the weekend. For now, he backed her against the wall and pushed his own jeans and boxers down over his hips.

She was doing a little jig, trying to step out of her jeans, but he could only wait long enough for her to free one foot. Once she had, he hooked his hand behind her knee and wrapped her leg around his waist.

"Oh!" She looked up and the surprise and desire he saw in her eyes pushed him over the edge. He slid his hand between her legs, not sure if she'd be ready. He needn't have worried. She was hot and wet. He tormented her clit, making her moan and rock her hips. He dipped a finger inside her and moaned himself as her velvety wetness tightened around it and grasped it tight. He withdrew his hand, needing to feel her grip his cock instead. He guided himself to her entrance and stroked her with his hard head. He couldn't help his smile as she grasped his ass and urged him inside. He thrust his hips and plunged deep, making them both gasp. "Oh, God, Antonio. Fuck me!"

Her choice of words startled him, but he was happy to oblige. She clung to him, and he gripped her leg around his waist. She was opened up perfectly for him, and he let her have it—deep and hard. Until now, he'd been restrained with her; he'd made love to her. Now she was begging him to fuck her, and he wasn't going to disappoint. He thrust his hips wildly, loving the feel of her as she moved with him, closing around him with each stroke. His breath was coming hard, and soon, so would he. The tension was building at the base of his spine, sending out ripples of pleasure each time he plunged inside her. He wasn't going to last. He needed to make her ...

"Oh. Oh. Oooh!" She leaned her head back against the wall and screamed at the ceiling as she tightened around him.

"Give it to me," he cried. His orgasm tore through him, sending waves of pleasure pulsating through his body and into hers. He saw stars as he drove deeper and harder, their bodies melding into one. He came hard, the waves crashing through him from the soles of his feet right up to his scalp. They moved together faster and faster and then more slowly, their orgasm like a crescendo that slowly receded, leaving them quivering in each other's arms.

When they were finally still, she looked up into his eyes. "Wow."

He let her leg down and carefully stepped back. "Well, you did ask me to fuck you."

She chuckled. "You can expect that to be a regular request in the future."

"I can? I'll happily oblige." His heart buzzed in his chest. Not only was it a request any guy would love to hear on a regular basis, but more than that, she was talking about their future.

~ ~ ~

Mary Ellen turned to look at him as he turned the car off the road. "Where are we going?"

He smiled but didn't answer.

She looked out the window, then back at him. "If I didn't know any better, I'd say we were going to the airport."

He shot her a quick smile. "Who says you do know any better?"

She frowned. "I don't know. I think I just assumed we'd be going to the coast."

"You want to go to the coast?"

She laughed. "I don't mind where we go. I just want to know where it is."

He chuckled as he turned into the airport. "You're telling me you don't like surprises?"

She thought about that for a moment. "No, I don't suppose I do. I like known factors, so that I can prepare for them."

He parked the car and turned to her. "Sometimes, I find it's better not to prepare. To go with the flow, you know? Spontaneity can be fun."

She nodded. "It can be, you're right." She smiled. "But would you please tell me where we're going?"

He laughed. "You don't want to try being spontaneous?"

"Maybe, soon, at something else. In fact, I think we were already spontaneous once this morning, so you have to give me some credit for that."

Shivers ran through her as he ran his gaze over her appreciatively. "I give you all the credit for that. So, fair's fair. My plan, if you want to do it, is to take you to Summer Lake."

"Oh."

"You don't like that idea?"

"I do. I've wanted to go see it for a while. It sounds like a wonderful place. It's just that I don't associate you with going there. It's where Piper came from. Where Cam met her. It's where Smoke and Laura live, but I never thought of you going there."

He smiled. "I haven't been there for years, but I have some very good friends there. Of course, there's my cousin, Cole—or Smoke, as everyone seems to call him these days. Did you know he and Marcos and I all went to college together?"

"I didn't."

"Yeah, and the guys Smoke works with now—at least the ones he leases his plane to, we met them in college, too. We've all been good friends ever since. Jack and Pete and Nate. I've wanted to get down there and visit them, and I know you've wanted to see the place."

Mary Ellen nodded. She'd imagined that they'd be spending a romantic weekend alone together—not going to visit his old friends.

"You don't like the idea? We don't have to go there. I've got the plane for the weekend. We can go anywhere you like."

She shrugged. "No. It'll be good. Just … tell me so I can know what to expect, are we going to visit your friends?"

"I thought we could visit with them, but only if you want to." He cupped her cheek in his hand. I want you to myself most of the time, but I'd like you to meet my friends, the people who are important to me. If you want to?"

Mary Ellen's heart beat a little faster at that. Here she'd been thinking that he was trying to kill two birds with one stone—spend some time with her and get to catch up with friends, but he was telling her he wanted her to meet the people who were important to him? That put a very different spin on things.

She smiled. "Yeah. I'd like that a lot."

"Good. I think you'll like them. They're good people, and I know they'll like you." He planted a kiss on her lips and got out of the car.

Mary Ellen watched out of the window as the plane descended over the hills. The lake shimmered blue and silver, growing bigger as they came in to land. The hills which had seemed so small beneath them just a few minutes ago, now rose up to welcome them, and by the time they touched down on the runway, they huddled around like protective giants. She loved the place already.

A golf cart came out to meet them on the tarmac and took them to the FBO building where Smoke greeted them with a smile.

Antonio embraced him in his usual enthusiastic manner. It made Mary Ellen smile that not only did he get away with his man hugs, but that even a guy as intense as Smoke embraced him back with a big grin.

"It's good to see you here finally."

Antonio grinned. "It's good to be here. Especially with Mary Ellen." He put his arm around her shoulders and drew her into his side.

Smoke nodded at her. "I'm glad to see you. Cam and Piper have both talked about getting you up here, but I'm even happier that you're here with this guy."

Mary Ellen smiled. She liked Smoke, but she never knew what to say to him.

"Don't take any crap from him, will you?"

She laughed out loud at that. "Oh, don't worry, there's no chance of that."

Antonio laughed with her, and Smoke looked a little taken aback.

Antonio hugged her closer to his side. "I should explain. Mary Ellen is not just a friend for the weekend. We're dating. I'm trying to impress her, because I hope that soon she'll agree to more than dating."

Smoke looked shocked at that, but not as shocked as Mary Ellen knew she must look.

Antonio grinned at them both. "I brought her here, so she can meet my friends."

Smoke shook his head in wonder and looked at Mary Ellen. "I'm assuming this isn't news to you?"

She chuckled. "Not exactly, no. I think of him the same way you do. I've known him for years, but it turns out he's not the guy I thought he was."

Antonio held his hands up. "If anyone knows how it goes, Smoke does." He turned to his cousin. "You lived the same life I did until you met Laura, right?"

Mary Ellen was amazed at the way Smoke's expression changed. He nodded and smiled and grasped Antonio's shoulder, then looked at her again. "I know exactly what he means now, but I'm not sure you do?"

She shrugged. She knew what he was saying. She knew Smoke's story, even if she didn't know him that well. He'd been another one who only spent time with women for one reason. Then he'd met Laura and changed his ways completely. He was now a one-woman-man and a devoted husband. "I know what he's saying; my problem is that I'm not sure I totally believe it."

Smoke raised an eyebrow. "All I can say is that I've known him all his life. He's a man of his word. He wouldn't say it if he didn't mean it. And ..." He hesitated, but then decided to go on. "If you think about it, he's never said it when he didn't mean it."

Mary Ellen wasn't sure she understood that.

Antonio gave her a rueful smile. "I think it's safe to spell it out, it's not as though you don't know who I've been. In the past, with women, there may have been many of them, but I never made them any promises. I never misled anyone about my intentions. I never pretended I wanted anything other than—" He stopped himself short, but they all knew he'd been about to say sex. "Than what I said," he finished, looking a little shamefaced.

"That's true." Mary Ellen was surprised to find herself more interested in letting him know that she wasn't offended, than she was in worrying about all the women he'd been with in the past. She smiled and dug him in the ribs. "I just have to hope that I'm not the first one you're subjecting to some new approach."

Smoke laughed.

"But, my darling, you are." Antonio gave her his best smile. "I'm experimenting with how I'm going to approach the rest of my life—but don't worry, you're not just the first, you're the one and only."

Smoke shook his head. "Okay. Enough. I'm getting out of the middle of this one. Your rental car is out in the lot. It's the red Buick, the keys are in it. Give me a call later and we'll see about meeting up." He smiled at Mary Ellen. "If you want to."

Chapter Twelve

Antonio went to stand on the balcony that overlooked the lake. Smoke had really done him a favor finding this place. His friend owned the resort and luckily the most expensive cabin had been available for the weekend. It was way too big for just the two of them, but that didn't matter. It was perfect. It stood in its own secluded little cove with an amazing view of the lake. It felt like they were completely isolated from the rest of the world, but it was only a few minutes back into the main resort area.

Antonio knew there was a restaurant there and Smoke had told him there'd be live music tonight. He'd spoken to Jack yesterday and he'd said that he and his wife Emma would be there tonight, as would Pete and his wife, Holly, and Nate and his fiancée, Lily. He smiled. They were all ahead of him on their life's journey. They'd already found their woman and managed to persuade her to spend her life with him. He'd found Mary Ellen, but he knew he needed to convince her that he was for real before he could ask her to spend her life with him. He hoped this weekend would help his cause. He'd been uncertain about bringing her here; he wanted her all to himself, but he wanted her to meet the guys, too. It was about making her a part of his life, and about letting her know that he wanted her to be a big part of it—the most important part. He hoped she'd understand. He'd thought about taking her to meet his parents, but that was a long way to go just for a weekend. He still planned to take her, but she might think this was too soon and he'd want more than a weekend anyway.

He turned as Mary Ellen came out to join him. "This place is spectacular," she said with a smile. "Thank you."

He shook his head. "Thank you for agreeing to come. I'm so happy I get to enjoy this beautiful place with my beautiful woman."

She smiled at him uncertainly.

"What don't you like about what I just said?"

She shrugged. "Your woman?"

He nodded vigorously. "That's what I want you to be."

She stared out at the lake, but didn't say anything.

"You don't believe me?"

She shrugged. "I kind of do." She came to him and leaned on the railing beside him. "It's weird. I've known you all this time, but never really knew you at all. It'd be easier if I could believe that I had you all wrong." She turned to look him in the eye. "But I didn't, did I?"

He bit the inside of his lip while he considered how he could best answer. He wanted to be honest; that was most important, but he wanted her to understand him. "In some ways, no. You know who I've been, you know how I've lived my life." He shrugged. "I can't tell you I'm ashamed of any of it. I had fun. I did no harm. I've always been honest."

She nodded and drew in a deep breath. "I know. I'm not judging you. I don't have a problem with any of it. I think my problem stems from the way I saw you, not from the way you were."

He gave her a puzzled look. "I'm not sure I want to hear the answer, but how did you see me?"

"I thought you were shallow. I thought you were superficial. I'm sorry. I judged you by your lifestyle. You went with so many women—but only incredibly attractive ones. You obviously weren't drawn to them for their personalities."

He chuckled. "Some of them were very nice people."

She dug him in the ribs with her elbow. "I'm sure they were, but you know what I mean. It seemed to me that you were all about the things that don't really matter in life, at least not to me. You were interested in looks and material things."

He pursed his lips. He didn't want to interrupt her to defend himself, but it was hard to hold his tongue.

"I mean, everything about you says you're wealthy and you like to spend your money on the finer things in life. Things that look good and cost a lot and ... I don't know. Status symbols." She turned to look him in the eye. "I thought that was what you were all about and it's totally not what I'm about."

He blew out a sigh. "What was your life like growing up?"

She shrugged. "Normal, I guess."

He smiled. "I think the way I grew up was normal, too, because to me it was. What does normal mean to you?"

She cocked her head to one side. "To me, it means middle-class, suburban, down-to-earth kind of living and good old-fashioned values. I grew up knowing you have to work hard to achieve anything in life. And whatever you do achieve, you appreciate and you're proud of." She gave him a puzzled look. "I'm not ashamed of where I come from. I'm proud of it."

He smiled. "And so you should be. I just wanted you to think about it a little. See, to me, the normal of growing up was being wealthy, living on two continents. Having a big extended family who are also wealthy, who work hard and reap the rewards. It was never down-to-earth living, but I was brought up on good old-fashioned values." He hesitated, wondering how he could make her see what he meant. "My point is that I grew up believing that having the best of everything is normal. And being the best at things is normal, too. When you think about how I've lived my life, you'll see that I've lived according to my normal. I like to have fun, and I have the means to have whatever kind of fun I want to. I only want the best." He shrugged. "Going out with lots of women was fun. In the circles I move in there are lots of women who are just out for a good time. Again, I only wanted the best. It may not have seemed like I was living any good old-fashioned values to you, but I was. As I said earlier, I never made any promises. I always made my intentions clear. I truly am a man of my word."

She gave him a grudging smile. "I can see that now, but looking at it from the outside, can you see how it looked to me?"

"Of course I can. I know most people see me that way—as shallow and arrogant. It didn't matter to me until now. I don't care what people think of me." He turned to face her. "But I care what you think. I want you to know who I am, in my heart. I want you to learn to believe in me. I want you to trust me and know my intentions are real."

She narrowed her eyes. "I think it's a little too soon for all of that."

He frowned. Did she mean it was too soon to trust him or too soon to talk about his intentions? It didn't really matter which. He'd just have to keep showing her, keep proving to her that he was for real.

She pushed away from the railing and smiled. "It's not too soon for lunch, though, is it? I'm starving. Do you want to take a walk into the resort? There was a restaurant on the little town square. I'd love to sit out on the deck over the water."

He smiled. She wanted to leave all the serious talk and get on with their weekend? That was fair. He took hold of her hand and led her back inside. "Let's go eat, then. And afterward, what would you like to do? We can rent a boat, go horseback riding, go for a hike, or ride four-wheelers ..."

"I prefer boats and hikes, but if you want to go for something with four legs or four wheels, I'll give it a try."

He chuckled. "I'm happier on two legs or in a boat, also. I just wanted to give you all the options I know of."

"Thanks." She let them out of the cabin and he closed the door behind them. "If we're going to be doing things together, you should probably know that I'm not overly adventurous. I'll try things if you want to do them, but if it's down to me I'll be happy going for a walk or sitting and talking over a glass of wine."

He smiled. "Or a Margarita?"

She laughed. "How did you know that?"

He tapped the side of his nose. "I pay attention."

~ ~ ~

Mary Ellen stared out at the lake and drew in a deep breath. "This place is even more beautiful than I pictured it."

Antonio nodded. "It's a good place. I haven't been here in far too long, but if you like it, we can start coming up on the weekends, maybe get ourselves a cabin."

Mary Ellen looked at him. He meant rent a cabin when they came, right? Not get a vacation home here like Cam and Piper had. She didn't get chance to ask him to explain as a guy approached their table.

"Antonio! It's good to see you; the guys said you were coming this weekend."

Mary Ellen liked the guy immediately. Antonio stood to shake his hand and then wrapped him in his customary hug. "Ben!

It's good to see you. I'd like to introduce you to my girlfriend, Mary Ellen."

Ben smiled and shook her hand. "It's nice to meet you. Welcome. How do you like the cabin?"

She smiled. "It's beautiful. I love the whole resort. It's a credit to you."

"Thank you." The way Ben smiled, she could tell the compliment meant a lot to him—and so it should. The resort was perfect in her eyes. From the wonderful cabin they were staying in, to the amazing scenery, to the deck where they were sitting over the water, Mary Ellen had already fallen in love with the place. "I can't really stop and chat right now—we're busy—but you guys are coming out tonight, aren't you?"

Antonio raised an eyebrow at her and Mary Ellen nodded. "We are. I'm looking forward to it."

"Good, I'll catch up with you then. The whole gang will be here, and I'm taking the night off so Charlie and I can have dinner with everyone."

Antonio grinned at him. "I'm happy everything worked out for the two of you."

Ben smiled. "Thanks, we got there in the end." He turned to Mary Ellen. "I'll introduce you to my wife later."

"Great. I'll look forward to it." Mary Ellen smiled as she watched him walk away. "He seems nice. Is he one of the guys you went to college with?"

"No, but he grew up here with one of them—Pete." He chuckled. "You'll probably like Pete the best."

"Oh, and why's that?"

He chuckled again. "Because I drive him nuts. He's like you, he'd rather plan than be spontaneous. He's organized and practical. He's the realist while his partner Jack is more of the idea man."

Mary Ellen smiled. "I'm sure I'll like them both."

"I hope you'll like them all—and their wives."

"Are they all married now?"

"Jack's married to Emma, who's a real sweetheart, and they have a baby girl—Isabel. I haven't met her yet; I can't wait."

Watching his face, Mary Ellen had to smile. He looked genuinely excited at the thought of meeting a baby.

"Pete is married to Holly," he continued, "and Nate is engaged to Lily. I haven't met her yet, but I'm curious to."

"And why's that?"

He met her gaze and a smile played on his lips. "If I'm honest, I'm curious to know what kind of woman could tame him. He was always something of a ladies' man."

Mary Ellen smiled. She was curious to meet Lily now, too; she wouldn't mind picking her brain about how it felt to date a guy who was known to play the field—and not only that, but how she'd navigated going from dating to engaged. She looked out at the lake again. Was it really a possibility that she and Antonio might go down that road? Who knew? It was far too early to tell.

After they'd eaten, they walked back to the cabin to collect the rental car. The resort was busy, and there were no boats available for the afternoon, so they'd booked one for the next day and were going out for a hike this afternoon.

"Do you know where you're going?" she asked as he pulled out of the resort and headed east.

"I do. The guys have a big development up on the other end of the lake. Smoke told me about some good hiking trails up there. I thought we could have a look around the place and then go for our walk."

"Great." She liked that he seemed to know his way around out here, even though he hadn't visited in years.

When they arrived at the resort at Four Mile Creek, Mary Ellen got out of the car and looked around. "I think I love it over here even more," she said with a smile. There was a big modern lodge and newer houses, some of them right down on the water's edge.

"I had a feeling you would. You might be a down-to-earth Midwestern girl, but your taste is more modern, right?"

She nodded. "I guess it is."

He put his arm around her shoulders and tucked his thumb under her chin and tilted her head, so she was looking into his eyes. "I already know you so well."

"It seems you do." It felt good that he did.

"If we get a place here, we should look at the ones on the water."

She narrowed her eyes at him, wondering if he'd explain what he meant. He could only mean rent one, couldn't he?

He shrugged and gave her a mischievous smile. "Are you ready to walk?"

She nodded.

"And what's it to be? Do you want to take a trail, or do you want to look around the shopping plaza first?"

She smiled through pursed lips. If he knew her so well, he should already know the answer to that.

He nodded and started walking her past the lodge to what looked like a little town square—there was even a clock tower overlooking the main area and a little café with a terrace outside. She loved it, and she loved that he really did know her.

"Did you know this is where Laura has her store?"

"Oh. I think I did, but I hadn't put two and two together."

"Do you want to go see if she's there?"

"Sure, why not." She liked Laura, and if they were visiting with people, it'd be nice to see a familiar face.

Antonio stopped when they reached the jewelry store and took his time browsing the window display. Mary Ellen loved looking at jewelry, though this was way out of her range. Laura had become a big name in the last few years, and her work carried the price tags to go with it.

"What's your favorite stone?" asked Antonio.

She shrugged. She liked them all and she didn't want him getting any ideas about buying her something—at least, not from here.

He gave her a stern look. "You have to tell me, otherwise it will be a surprise, and I already know you don't like those."

She shook her head. "You don't need to get me anything."

"I know, but I want to. Can I?" He held her gaze. It felt like he was asking other, bigger questions, too. Did she trust him? Would she allow him to do something nice for her? Did she have hang-ups about money? She looked back into his big brown eyes, and all she could see in them was that same care and concern she'd seen that first night at Molly's.

What the hell? "Yes, if you want to. Thank you."

His face relaxed into a smile and he cupped her face between his hands and landed a kiss on her lips. "Thank you." He turned back to the window display. "Not a ring, not just yet." She sucked in a sharp breath, but he just shot her a mischievous smile. "I've seen you wear earrings, and a necklace sometimes, but never a bracelet. Don't you like them?"

She shrugged. "I do, but I don't have any."

"A bracelet, then?"

"Whatever you like." It felt weird. She'd like whatever he got her; in fact, that was an understatement. She'd treasure whatever he got her—forever.

He studied the display for a few more moments. "Does anything grab you? Do you see anything you want?"

She shook her head. There was a thin silver chain, that looked like it might cost less than anything else, but she knew he'd be onto her if she suggested that. "Surprise me?"

He chuckled. "But you don't like surprises."

"I don't mind them, especially when I don't have to prepare for them or pack accordingly."

He smiled and took her hand and led her inside.

The girl behind the counter greeted them with a smile. "Good afternoon. Can I help you with anything?"

"Good afternoon. Is Laura here?"

"I'm sorry, she's not. Can I take a message for her?"

"That's fine, Maria. We'll see her this evening."

Mary Ellen wondered if he knew the girl, but then she noticed her name tag.

"While we're here, though, could we see tray thirty-three from the front window?"

"Of course." Maria got her keys out and went to fetch the tray for them.

Mary Ellen gave him a puzzled look. She'd been looking at tray thirty-two and had assumed he was, too. That tray was full of link bracelets. The others were fancier with precious stones.

Maria came back and set the tray on the counter in front of them. Mary Ellen's eyes widened. They were some serious bracelets! She looked at him, but Antonio just smiled and pointed at one. "Could we see that?"

Mary Ellen shook her head slightly. It wasn't a bracelet, it was a cuff—encrusted with diamonds, sapphires, rubies, and emeralds. It was obscene! Ridiculously, beautifully obscene.

Maria took it out and smiled at her. "Would you like to try it?"

Mary Ellen looked at him and he nodded hopefully.

She held out her wrist and Maria fastened it on her. It was beautiful. She loved it, but what had she said to him about not being into material things? She looked at him uncertainly and he smiled. "It's perfect, we'll take it."

Mary Ellen cringed, dreading hearing how much it cost.

"Do you want to wear it now?" asked Maria.

She shook her head. She'd be scared to death to lose it.

Antonio looked sad. "You don't love it?"

"I do. It's beautiful, it's just I think I should save it for best."

He gave her his sexiest smile. "You think there are better times than right here and right now?"

She relaxed and smiled back. "Probably not."

Maria was watching them with a sappy smile on her face. "I'll get you the box."

Antonio followed her to the front where she put a beautiful ornate box into a bag for him. Mary Ellen smiled to herself at the thought that she would have been thrilled if the box itself had been the gift. She busied herself looking at the displays while Maria rang him up, not wanting to hear how much she'd just cost him.

Once they were back out on the street, he took hold of her hand and held it up, so he could admire the bracelet.

"Thank you." She smiled. "It's beautiful."

"You deserve beautiful. Thank you for letting me. I wasn't sure you would."

She reached up and planted a kiss on his lips. "Neither was I. It was hard for me to do that, but I know it's part of who you are, and ..."

"And what?" He looked worried.

She smiled. "I can always give it back when you break up with me." She didn't know if she expected him to look relieved or frustrated when she said that. Whatever she'd expected, he surprised her. He smiled happily. "Good."

"Good?"

He chuckled. "Because I don't ever want it back."

His words sent shivers down her spine as he held her gaze, and, for the first time, she believed him.

Chapter Thirteen

"Have I told you how beautiful you are?" Mary Ellen took his breath away as she came down the stairs. She'd been so quick getting ready that he'd thought she must be coming down for something she'd forgotten. As far as Antonio could see, she hadn't forgotten a damned thing. She was wearing a long orange and yellow skirt that skimmed her feet. It covered everything, yet accentuated her figure perfectly. Her top was an off-the-shoulder number, white and demure, yet it featured her full breasts and only had him wanting to undress her here and now instead of taking her out to show her off.

She smiled when she reached the bottom. "Not in the last hour or so. You can tell me again if you like. I love hearing it."

He got to his feet and went to her, placing his hands on her waist as he let his gaze travel over her. He drew in a deep breath, resisting the urge to pull her against him. "You, Mary Ellen, are beautiful. You're perfect."

She laughed. "I'm a long way from perfect; for starters, there's far too much of me to be perfect. Did you know I was on a diet when we started seeing each other? I need to get back to that soon. But, since beauty is in the eye of the beholder, I'll take the beautiful part, thank you."

He shook his head with a frown. "Please don't go on a diet. I love you just the way you are." He realized what he'd said as soon as he said it, and held his breath, waiting for her reaction. She didn't seem to notice, or if she did, she ignored it. "I have to go on a diet. I'll only keep getting bigger if I don't."

He shook his head and tightened his hands around her waist. "I've already told you I wish there was more of you. You're curvy. A man wants something to fill his hands with." He slid his hands around to cup her ass and smiled. "Perfect."

She wasn't going for it. "You might like to fill your hands with it, but you know what they say, more than a handful's a waste, and most men don't like big."

He scowled. "Then most men are crazy. And why does it matter to you what they like?" He bit his lip as soon as he'd said it. He knew it could come across as jealous or possessive, and he supposed, in a way, it was. He didn't want her to care what other men liked. He wanted her to be happy that he loved her body, that to him she was perfect.

She narrowed her eyes at him. "I wasn't saying it matters to me; I was simply saying what's normal. Are you ready to go?"

He hesitated for a moment. He wanted to push it. He wanted to make her understand how he felt, but there was no point. He'd have to take his time and make her see that he meant what he said, and all he could do was wait and hope that one day the way he saw her would be more important to her than what most men thought.

He nodded. "Do you want to walk to the Boathouse?"

She smiled, and all the tension left him. "Yeah, shall we? That way we can have a romantic walk back in the moonlight."

He nodded, liking that idea, and wondering whether they'd make it back to the cabin before he could undress her. He'd love to see her naked in the moonlight—to make love under the stars.

She snapped her fingers in front of his face. "Did I lose you? You just zoned out on me."

He gave her a guilty smile. "I was thinking about what we might do before we get back here."

She looked at him in surprise. "Outside?"

He nodded. He could tell the thought turned her on. "If you want to? Under the moonlight. On the beach?"

She nodded eagerly. "Or maybe here, on the deck, so we can run for cover if someone comes?"

He chuckled. "Someone will come, all right."

She laughed. "You know what I mean."

"I do. Leave it to me. I'll think of something."

She reached up and planted a kiss on his lips. "Let's not stay out too late then."

"No? Why not?" He wanted to hear her say that the idea turned her on. He wanted her to tell him that she wanted him. "Does it turn you on?"

She nodded and dropped her gaze. He titled her chin up so she had to look him in the eye. "Do I turn you on?"

She nodded again. "You always have."

"I have?" That was a pleasant surprise. "I wouldn't have believed you thought of me in that way before last weekend."

She gave an embarrassed laugh and stepped away from him. "Believe me, you have no idea." She picked up her purse and let herself out of the cabin before he could catch up and ask her what she meant.

~ ~ ~

Mary Ellen looked around the large group they were sitting with. She loved it! She loved this place. The resort was even better at night than it had been during the day. The restaurant opened up onto the deck over the water. The band had set up on a little stage under the stars. Moonlight reflected off the water behind them. It was awesome. She loved Antonio's friends. She felt at home with them straight away and was amazed that, in such a large group, there was no one she didn't like. They were an odd group, to say the least. All very different people, but the vibe of the group was wonderful. There was such warmth and friendship; she'd swear she could feel it in the air around them.

Antonio had introduced her to his buddies and their wives. She could see why they were friends. Jack, Pete, and Nate were all good-looking, confident men—and they all seemed to know a lot about wine. She liked their wives. Emma was a sweetie who seemed to be quite taken with Antonio—and made no secret of it. Holly was cool, and Mary Ellen could see what Antonio had meant about Pete being a planner and organizer. She liked him, but she felt for Holly. She reminded Mary Ellen that perhaps she should go easier on Cameron at work. Lily was maybe her favorite, if only because of the way she was with her fiancé Nate. He was super hot and a real charmer. Antonio had told her that he used to be a real ladies' man, but Lily was obviously confident in his affection, and anyone with eyes in their head couldn't miss how hopelessly in love with her he was.

She turned to look at Antonio. He was chatting with Dan, Jack's brother, who was some kind of computer genius. Was it possible that he might feel like that about her someday—and that she could ever feel as confident about him as Lily did about Nate? She shook her head slightly. That seemed like a big ask.

Missy, Dan's wife, caught her eye from across the table. "Are you doing okay, hon?"

Mary Ellen nodded at her. Of all of them, Missy was the one she related to the most. She was down-to-earth and spoke her mind. "I'm great, thanks."

Missy nodded. "Good. It can get a bit overwhelming when we're all out together."

Mary Ellen smiled. "I'm not one to get overwhelmed much."

Missy laughed. "Good. You're going to have to get used to us if you and your husband buy a place up here."

Mary Ellen shook her head rapidly. "We're not married."

"Oh!" Missy looked shocked. "Oh. Sorry. I thought ..." She shook her head. "Don't mind me. I got the wrong end of the stick."

Antonio turned and put his arm around Mary Ellen's shoulders. "Please, don't apologize, Missy. In fact, keep talking. The more she hears it, the more she might get used to the idea."

Mary Ellen turned to look up at him. He was joking, right? No. He had that look in his eyes again. He looked like he cared about her. Like he cared what she thought. Like what she thought about what he was saying right now might be very important to him. She smiled uncertainly, and he dropped a kiss on her lips. "Think about it."

She didn't get chance to reply.

Emma was standing behind her, tapping her on the shoulder. "Do you want to come and dance?"

Mary Ellen looked around. Most of the girls were heading to the dance floor. Missy grinned at her from across the table. "Come on."

Antonio held her gaze for a moment. She couldn't describe the look in his eyes, but she knew for certain he was serious. He wasn't messing with her. All she had to figure out now was one, if she could allow herself to trust him, and two, this tiny detail of how she really felt about him. She'd had a crush on him forever. She knew he was good-looking. She knew she liked the guy he was turning out to be, but did that mean she was ready for something serious? Something as serious as him

being her husband? She shuddered as she followed Missy and
Emma out onto the dance floor. She loved the idea in her
heart, but her practical mind would need to think long and
hard about the reality.

~ ~ ~

Jack grasped Antonio's shoulder and grinned at him. "So,
you're about to join the rest of us?"
He shrugged.
"What do you mean, you don't know?" asked Pete. "It's plain
as day, you're besotted with her."
Antonio nodded and blew out a sigh. "I am, I'm not denying
that. But, since you're so knowledgeable about these things, do
you think she feels the same way about me?"
Nate laughed. "You're not serious? You, the great Antonio Di
Giovanni, aren't sure if a woman's into you? I thought it went
without saying. Look at you. If I weren't engaged, I'd be
throwing my panties at you. You're like your wines—you just
get better with age."
Antonio had to laugh. "Thanks, Nate. It's good to know you
still love me. Or at least you'd jump into bed with me if you
were a girl, but that's kind of the point, isn't it? There's a
difference. Is she into me? Yeah, sure, she is." He swaggered
his shoulders, making them laugh. "I've still got it. But I want
more than that, and that's new territory for me. Just because
she's into me, that doesn't mean she wants more with me—
does it? I mean, I've been into a lot of women …"
Nate laughed. "You can say that again."
Antonio sighed. "I know, I know, but I wouldn't have wanted
anything serious with any of them. What if she feels that way
about me? That I'm good for a quick bang, but that's it?"
The others all stared at him. No one spoke for a few moments.
Which made him wonder. Was it true? Could they all see it?
That she wasn't into him for anything meaningful?

He looked around at them all hopefully. To his surprise, the one who spoke up was Jack's younger brother, Dan. He smiled at him shyly and nodded. "These guys don't seem to have anything to say—for once. So, I'll tell you what I think. I don't think you've got anything to worry about. At least not about what she'd like to happen. You only need to watch, and you'll understand. She's into you in a physical way, but that's easy to judge." He smiled. "It seems to me you have enough experience with that to figure it out for yourself. But as for the two of you as people, she looks to you for reassurance—she looks to you before she answers questions. She looks at you when you're talking to other people. She wants to know what you have to say, and she wants to be part of what you're talking about. My guess is that she wants something serious with you, but she's afraid to trust it. She doesn't think you're into being serious with anyone, and she doesn't see herself as the only person in the world you could possibly get serious about."

Antonio stared at him for a long moment. He didn't know Dan as well as the others, but he'd met him a few times over the years and respected his mind—he respected him even more in this moment.

Jack grinned at them. "If that's what Dan says, then that's how it is. He's the smartest one amongst us."

The others nodded.

"Yeah." Nate grinned at Dan. "He knows a damned sight more about women than I ever will."

Antonio raised an eyebrow at that and Dan smiled at him. "I don't know even a tiny percentage of what Nate knows in one respect, but I don't think you need any help in that area either. But you guys who've always been good with the ladies seem to forget that they're people, too. They're not a different species, although it can seem that way sometimes." They all laughed at that. "You're feeling unsure and insecure? You can bet she is, too. She's finding her way just like you are, not knowing if you're for real, or if she's going to get hurt. The best thing you can do is treat her as your best friend. You're not a man and a woman playing some chess game and trying to win each other's hearts. You're just two people trying to make their way through life and find happiness. All you can do is share everything, talk to each other, help each other and support each other." He stopped and looked around at the others who were all staring at him. "That's what I think, anyway, and now you can all start giving me shit."

Pete blew out a sigh. "No one's going to give you any shit, Danny. I think I can speak for all of us when I say that we're wondering how you got so smart and wondering why, even though we know it, we forget that stuff sometimes."

Dan shrugged and took a drink of his beer. "We forget when we let other things get in the way—when we let work or life become more important. I'm just lucky, I guess. From the day I asked Miss to marry me, I swore to myself that I would never let anything be more important to me than her and Scotty."

Antonio had to swallow around the lump in his throat as he nodded. "Thanks, Dan."

The others nodded and mumbled their thanks, too. Jack lifted his glass in a toast. "Here's to my little brother, the smartest guy and most unlikely agony aunt in the world."

They all laughed as they raised their glasses and the emotion of the moment passed, but Antonio was fairly sure that he wasn't the only one on whom Dan's words would leave a lasting impression.

~ ~ ~

Despite having said they should leave early, they closed the place down, and Mary Ellen was sad to leave at the end of the night. It was the best night she'd had in a long time. She'd made a whole bunch of new friends—friends that she wanted to keep in touch with and get to know better, not just some passing acquaintances who happened to be married to Antonio's friends. She hugged each and every one of them before they left.

"You'd better be back soon," said Missy. "I'll have to come hunt you down otherwise, and I hate to fly, just ask Smoke."

Smoke laughed. "Yeah, do me a favor, Mary El? Come back, anything other than make me fly this one around."

Laura laughed as Missy wrinkled her nose at him. "Hey. You're supposed to be nice and reassuring, remember? Not bitch about me."

Smoke held his hands up. "Sorry, Miss, it's been a long night. I just want to get my lady home."

Emma stepped forward for another hug. "Yeah, we have to get going now, too. Jack's mom's watching Isabel for us and I don't like to be too late, but you've got my number. Call me, and come back soon, okay?"

Mary Ellen nodded happily.

Pete grasped Antonio's shoulder as he smiled at her. "And do us all a favor and put this guy out of his misery?"

Everyone turned and stared at him as though he'd put his foot in it, big time. Pete laughed. "I mean, he wants to buy a house here, help him pick one out, would you?"

Everyone laughed, but Mary Ellen didn't miss the look of relief on Antonio's face at Pete's explanation.

Laura came and hugged her. "This was so much fun. I hope you do come back soon, but I'll be over to see Piper next week, so we can catch up then." She leaned in closer and spoke quietly. "If you want to be, I think you'll be part of the family before long."

Mary Ellen didn't know what to say. She smiled and nodded but had no words. They all seemed to think that she and

Antonio were going to get together for real, for serious—she wasn't sure she even wanted to think it out loud—that they'd get married?! Shivers ran down her spine. It was so far-fetched, and yet at the same time, it seemed so right. Until she remembered that less than two weeks ago she'd still thought of him as an arrogant prick.

Chapter Fourteen

Antonio took hold of her hand as they walked down the path to the water's edge. It would lead them past all the little coves and beaches and back to the cabin. At the beginning of the night, he'd been looking forward to their walk home—looking forward to getting her naked and making love to her again. Now, that part seemed less important. He knew he could make love to her; he knew they'd both enjoy it. What he wasn't sure of was whether he could make her fall in love with him. Did anyone ever make someone fall in love with them? Or did it just happen of its own accord? If it did, wouldn't she feel it by now—like he did? He already knew he was in love with her. Seeing her tonight had only confirmed it for him. Watching her dance with the girls, talk business with Laura and Holly, talk babies with Emma. He sighed. She was at home with all of them. She was everything he wanted.

"Are you okay?" She looked worried. "That was a big sigh. Did you have a good time tonight?"

He wrapped his arm around her shoulders as they walked. "I had a wonderful time. It was good to see them all again. I love this place, I love being here, but the best part of all was being here with you. Did you enjoy it?"

She smiled. "I had a great time, and I agree with everything you said. I love it here, I love the people, I love the place, but the best part was being here with you."

He drew in a deep breath and stopped walking. Taking hold of both of her hands, he turned to face her.

"What's wrong?" She looked worried again.

"Nothing. Nothing's wrong. Everything's wonderful, but there's something I need to ask you."

She looked cautious. "What?"

"You said you love it here. You love the people. You love the place." He hesitated. Was he really going to ask her? Wasn't it too soon? Wasn't he supposed to be taking it slowly? He was, but dammit, he didn't want to. He couldn't wait. He needed to know. "Do you think you could ever love me?"

Her eyes widened, and her lips parted in surprise. By her reaction, it really was too soon, but at the same time, it was too late now—he's asked. He'd get to hear her answer whether he liked it or not.

She didn't speak for a long moment. He wanted to say something. To save her and himself from the awkward truth, but he made himself keep quiet. He had to hear it from her.

Eventually she blew out a big sigh, and then, to his surprise, she nodded slowly. She looked up into his eyes and nodded again. "Honestly? Yes. I do think I could. In fact, I'll be completely honest with you, Antonio, I know I could fall in love with you."

His chest buzzed with happiness and he could feel his heart race. "You do? You are? Mary Ellen ..." He cupped her face between his hands. "I don't want to scare you away, but I have to tell you. I love you."

She bit her lip, but he could see she was smiling around it.

"When I told you you're perfect, I meant you're perfect for me. You're everything I want in this life, and I want to share it with you." He lifted her hands to his lips and kissed them. "I've tried to be patient. I waited as long as I could. I didn't want to scare you away."

To his surprise, she laughed. "This is patient? This is as long as you can wait?"

He nodded uncertainly. She was laughing at him?

She surprised him again by bringing their joined hands up to her lips, so she could kiss his knuckles. "You beautiful, ridiculous man. We've been seeing each other for one whole week. Do you know how crazy it sounds?"

"I do. I know, but it's true. It's not like we were strangers when we met. We've known each other for a long time, and the heart doesn't know time in the same way the mind does. The heart just knows."

She looked shocked, as though he'd said something horribly wrong.

"What? What's wrong?"

To his relief she smiled and shook her head, then she laughed, almost in disbelief. "My mind has been trying to stick with the conventional sense of time, and I'll be honest, it's been trying to protect my heart, too. But I just remembered something that I told both Cameron and Chelsea recently."

"What?"

"I told them that falling in love isn't a decision that you make with your head according to some predetermined timeline. It's something that happens inside your heart that you can neither control nor deny."

He grinned at her. "Then there's our answer."

She nodded slowly, but she didn't look convinced.

"You don't think so?" His heart was racing again, but this time with fear—fear that she might change her mind already, tell him it was some mistake, that she could never love him.

She smiled and kissed his hand again. "I do think so. It's just … you know how I work. My mind likes to be in charge; it likes predetermined timelines and being in control. I can't deny what I feel, but I'm not used to listening to my heart—no matter how right it might be."

He nodded and drew her to him, wrapping her in a hug that for once wasn't about getting his body as close to hers as possible. This was about getting his heart closer to hers. "I understand. You need time, and you can take all the time you want, but now I have hope. I know that we're heading where I want to go."

She looked up at him. "Just so I'm sure about this and so I don't second-guess myself later when I'm alone and get to thinking that I made all of this up, where do you want this to go?"

"I want you to marry me, Mary Ellen. I want you to live with me and be my wife. I want us to have babies and grandchildren and grow old together. Oh, and I want us to buy a house here, so we can come visit whenever we like."

She laughed. "I'm glad you added that last part—take the pressure off a little, why don't you?"

"The rest feels like pressure?"

"No. Not really. It's just a lot to take in."

"I know, but if it's what we both want, then why waste time? We should get started on our life together as soon as we can. In fact …" He knew he was getting carried away, this wasn't taking it slow by any stretch of the imagination, but he couldn't help it. "When we go back, why don't you move in with me? You already spent every night with me. It was good, don't you think?"

She nodded. "It was good, but ..." She shook her head. "Give me some time to get my head around it? Part of me loves the idea—but another part of me wants to run away screaming. It's all happening too fast. If we really do have the rest our lives to figure it out, why not take a little time to get it right?"

He nodded. "I'm sorry. You're right. We should take all the time you need. I just need you to know that it's what I want. It's not lines or bullshit. This is for real, Mary Ellen. My love for you is real, and I promise you, it will last a lifetime."

Her eyes filled with tears as she looked up at him. "You have no idea how much I want to believe that."

He closed his arms around her. "But you don't yet, and that's okay. I have a lifetime to convince you that it's true.

~ ~ ~

The next morning, they decided to take a picnic up to Four Mile and hike one of the trails that Smoke had told them about last night. Mary Ellen wanted to explore and get to know more of the area since it looked like she'd be coming back here. She stared out of the window as Antonio drove them up past the new lodge and shopping plaza they'd visited yesterday. It was a lot to take in. Antonio Di Giovanni had told her that he was in love with her—and that he wanted to marry her, just as soon as she was ready. She hadn't slept too well last night; she'd kept turning it over and over in her mind. What was she waiting for? What time did she need? In the last ten days, her fantasy guy had suddenly morphed into a really great guy who loved her and wanted to marry her. Why wasn't she planning a wedding already? She sighed. She'd planned a wedding once before. Maybe that had something to do with it. She'd put in so much time and hard work, trying to make sure that everything would be perfect, and it all seemed to be working out wonderfully—right up until the point where David had dumped her. Of course, she'd been the one who'd had to clean up the mess. She'd had to make all the calls to cancel all the arrangements. The chapel, the florist, the caterers. She shuddered at the memory. All those people who'd tried to sound sympathetic to her situation, while still making it clear that she wouldn't be getting any money back.

Antonio reached across and took hold of her hand. "Are you okay, bella? Why so sad?"

She shook her head. She could hardly tell him what she was thinking about.

He parked the car at the trailhead and retrieved the backpack with their picnic supplies from the back seat. "Ready?"

She nodded, and they set out up the trail. It seemed that there had been a lot of work done recently to make the area around the trailhead into a park. There was a new restroom building by the parking area and a small pond surrounded by picnic benches.

Antonio raised an eyebrow at her. "Would you rather we stay here?"

Mary Ellen looked over at the benches. She wasn't much of an adventurer or a hiker, but she didn't want to stay in this man-made area. She wanted to go up the hillside, at least a little way, and see the amazing views of the lake Smoke had told them about. She shook her head. "No, let's go on up." She could tell by the way he smiled that that was his preference. As they passed the pond, she stopped and stared.

"What is it?"

She shook her head in wonder. "I think it's a magnolia." He followed her gaze to a small tree with big pink and white waxy flowers. She made her way over to it and smiled. "It is. Wow. I would never have believed that they'd grow here."

Antonio looked lost and she smiled at him. "Don't worry about it. They're my favorite trees. My grandad retired to South Carolina, and he had several of them in his yard when I was small. I loved them. I always wanted one but until I came to Napa I never lived anywhere where they'd grow. Of course, in Napa I can't have one either." She shrugged and gave him a rueful smile. "Sorry. Let's carry on. It just caught my eye."

They set off up the path again and soon they reached a clearing high up above the trees. The view was spectacular. The lake was laid out before them, shimmering blue surrounded by green hills.

Antonio took hold of her hand. "We need to buy a house here."

"I agree. You should." She might love the idea of coming here on weekends and for vacations. She might love the idea of coming here with him even more, but the idea of them buying a house here was just a little too far-fetched. He narrowed his eyes at her, but fortunately he let it go.

He selected a spot for them under the shade of some trees and spread the blanket out. The picnic was wonderful. That Ben guy ran the resort well. They'd been able to call the restaurant this morning and put in their order and then pick it up on their way out. The backpack was insulated, and everything was chilled with ice packs. Antonio unpacked sandwiches and salads and nuts and fruit. There was a bottle of water and a bottle of wine, too.

Mary Ellen picked up the wine. It didn't look familiar. "A Marsala?"

Antonio grinned. "I asked them to put it in. Do you like?"

She nodded. "I think so. I tend to think of it as a cooking wine—and in case you haven't noticed yet, I don't cook much."

He chuckled. "I had wondered about that. At least it means we won't fight over the kitchen. I love to cook. So, you can sit and drink wine and keep me company while I do."

She nodded. She loved that idea. He was hot, sexy, kind, compassionate. He claimed he was in love with her—and he cooked too? Did it get any better than that?

He smiled and opened the bottle. "Mostly, I use it for cooking. That drunken chicken we never got around to eating that first night you came to my place …"

"Oh!" She laughed. "Chicken Marsala. I should have known."

He nodded. "Sicilians are proud of our wines, especially the Marsala. Most people think of it as merely a cooking wine these days, but there are still some fine examples. It's like a sherry, a sweet fortified wine—good for dessert."

She had to smile. His passion for his wines was evident. She loved that about him.

They ate their sandwiches in companionable silence looking out at the lake—blue water dotted with white boats mirrored the blue sky above dotted with white clouds.

When she'd finished eating, she smiled at him. He was quieter today and she had a feeling that he was nervous about their conversation last night. "I could get used to this."

He grinned. "I hope you'll want to."

She nodded. "I do want to, Antonio. It's all so fast and a little hard to take in."

He nodded solemnly. "Hard to believe for you, I guess. You know me to be a certain way and that isn't as a guy who's looking to find the love of his life and settle down."

She nodded, glad that he understood.

"I know that with time I can show you who I am; I can earn your respect." He frowned. "Do you want to know what I'm not so sure about?"

"What?"

"I know I can do my part to prove to you that I'm for real, but I don't know that I can ever get you past the hurt you've known. Some people never trust again after they've had their heart broken."

She reached up and touched his cheek. "I don't think you've got much to worry about there."

"No?"

She smiled. "No. David did a number on me, I'm not denying that, but the way I've been since then has been more of a logical choice to avoid hurt, than an emotional need or fear of getting hurt."

He looked puzzled.

She shrugged. "He knocked me down, but he didn't destroy me. I was able to work through my hurt, and I made a conscious decision not to put myself out there to experience it again. I'm not some broken fearful woman. I'm perfectly capable of choosing to trust again—to love again. It's just a matter of risk versus reward."

He smiled and planted a kiss on her lips. "I'll do everything I can to minimize the risk and maximize the reward."

Mary Ellen sipped her wine and stared out at the lake. A big part of her already trusted that he meant it.

Chapter Fifteen

"I can't believe we're in for another laid-back Monday." Daniel eyed Antonio warily. "You have seen the numbers from Sicily, right? You're not just blissfully unaware?"

Antonio gave his assistant a half smile. "I've seen them. I know it's not good, but me throwing my arms in the air and ranting and raving isn't going to make them any better, is it?"

Daniel shook his head. "I know that. It's usually me telling you that, but damn, Antonio. Things are going down the pan over there. What's going on with Marcos? It's not like him to let things slip this badly."

Antonio shook his head sadly. "He's finally getting divorced. I'm sure he has a lot on his mind and a lot to deal with." He didn't like to add that he was more concerned about what Marcos had said last time they spoke—about maybe not getting his passion for the wines back. If he didn't—and if it didn't happen soon—Antonio was going to have to step in. He had no intention of going home to take things over, but he might have to visit for a while until the business was back on track, and either Marcos was back on form or they found someone to replace him.

"I'm sure he does, but still ..." Daniel looked uncomfortable. "It's going to make things more difficult for us."

"It is." Antonio smiled. "But, hey, we're good. We can handle it. If my brother needs us to pick up the slack for a while, we're up to the task, right?"

Daniel blew out a sigh. "Of course we are. We can handle it." He met Antonio's gaze. "I take it you had a good weekend? You're not phased at all, are you?"

Antonio grinned. "It was the best weekend ever, and no, I'm not phased, because I know my life is coming together, so a little road bump with the business isn't a big deal."

"You took her to Summer Lake, didn't you?"

"Yeah. It was amazing. In fact, can you find me a realtor up there? I want to start looking."

Daniel laughed. "Are you serious? The shit's hitting the fan here and you want to start looking for a vacation home?"

"I do." He turned back to his computer. "And do you know of any good nurseries?"

Daniel looked totally confused. "Nurseries? You mean for kids or for plants?"

Antonio laughed. "Just plants—for now."

"Yeah. I do, as a matter of fact. I took my dad to one just yesterday. Why?"

"I need to buy a magnolia tree."

Daniel ran both his hands through his hair. "If this is what love does to a man, then I hope it never strikes me. If I promise to track you down a magnolia tree by the end of the week, will you please focus and sit down with me to figure out how we're going to cover the losses on the Sicilian distribution?"

"Sure." Antonio smiled. "Let's do that." He wasn't nearly as worried as Daniel seemed to think he should be. It would be easy enough to turn things around at the winery at home. He'd step in if he had to, but first he wanted to talk to Marcos and his parents and find out what was going on.

~ ~ ~

Mary Ellen popped her head around Cameron's door. "Hey."

"Hey, yourself. Come on in. How was your weekend?"

"It was great. How was yours?"

"Quiet. We kicked back at home and made the most of some downtime."

She smiled. "And you didn't harass Piper too much with wedding plans?"

Cam pursed his lips. "No. I didn't. I'm starting to think she doesn't want to marry me."

"Don't be ridiculous. That's crazy talk."

"Is it? She never wants to talk about the wedding."

Mary Ellen shook her head. "Wanting to marry you and wanting to have a big wedding aren't the same thing, you know."

Cameron frowned. "You think she doesn't want the big wedding? She keeps saying she's fine with it. I'm only doing it for her."

Mary Ellen shrugged. "It's not my place to stick my nose in, but that's never stopped me before. Think about it; she's not a big, formal event kind of girl. It's not where she comes from and it's not like she has anyone she can invite to share it with her."

"It's for us to share together."

Mary Ellen rolled her eyes. "You do well most of the time, Cam. But you're still a guy. For a girl, a wedding is a big deal.

Either we dream about it and want something big and grand, or we want something simple and special to us. Whichever it is, we want to share it with our people—the ones who mean the most to us. Yes, of course, the guy that we're marrying, but also our friends and family. The people who've known us all our lives. Piper doesn't have anyone like that. She has no brothers or sisters. Her mom's gone. The only person who's known her all her life is Laura, and even she kind of belongs on your side now, because she's married to Smoke."

Cameron rested his elbows on his desk and his chin on his hands. "So, you're saying that the wedding will be full of all my people and she won't have anyone? And that that won't feel good to her?"

"I shouldn't be saying anything at all. I could be completely wrong, but if she's not enthusiastic about all your wedding plans, then I think you should sit her down and talk to her and find out why."

Cameron smiled. "You're right. I will. I want it to be perfect for her."

Mary Ellen grinned at him. "You're a good guy, Cam."

He laughed. "Thanks. And while we're on the subject of weddings …" He let his words trail off and raised an eyebrow. "What about them?"

"What about you? I talked to Chelsea yesterday and she's convinced that you and Antonio are headed in that direction. I told her it was way too soon to start thinking like that. Then, last night, Piper talked to Laura, and she seemed to think the same thing. Laura even said that Antonio wants to buy a house up there so the two of you can go back since you had so much fun."

She shrugged. "I don't know what to tell you, Cam. We had an amazing weekend. I love that place. Everyone's so nice. We had a lot of fun out on Saturday night with them."

"Stop avoiding it. What about you and Antonio?"

She shrugged again. "It could go in that direction."

Cameron grinned. "Yeah? That's fantastic." His grin faded. "But aren't things moving a little fast?"

She nodded her head vigorously. "I know! It's ridiculous to even be thinking about it."

"Is it? I seem to remember you told me that when it comes to love there are no predetermined timelines. It just happens and there's nothing you can do about it."

She blew out a sigh. "I know. It was easy for me to spout that stuff when it was about you and Piper or Chelsea and Grant, but now it's me. I need my timelines; I need known factors." She laughed. "I need to be in control, dammit."

Cam laughed with her. "You still can be in control. I find you only lose control when you resist what's happening. When you accept it and work with it, then you're still in control. Right?"

She mulled that over. "So, you're saying that instead of fighting it or denying it, I could just admit that it's happening and go along with the whirlwind?"

"Yep. I don't see why not. If it seems inevitable that you'll end up together, then you can either waste a bunch of time doubting it and fighting it first, or you can get with the program and roll with it from the outset."

She smiled. "I think I like that idea."

Cam smiled back. "So, you think it's inevitable that the two of you will end up together."

She drew in a deep breath and nodded. "It's starting to look that way."

They both turned at the sound of a knock on the door. It was Zoe, with another bunch of flowers, and a big smile.

"These just came for you, Mary Ellen."

She couldn't hide her smile. He'd sent her magnolias. She took them, but Zoe lingered in the doorway.

"I'm not going to read the card to you, so you may as well get back out to reception," she said with a laugh.

"Sorry." Zoe didn't look sorry at all, just disappointed that she didn't get to be nosey.

When she'd gone, Cameron grinned at Mary Ellen. "You don't get rid of me so easily. What does it say?"

She laughed. "I don't know yet. I haven't opened it, have I?"

"So, hurry up. What kind of flowers are they? They look expensive. I don't think I've ever seen those before."

She brought her hand up to her mouth to try to hide her smile. Antonio did pay attention. He'd claimed that when he knew about her secret Margarita habit, and he'd proved it with the flowers. "They're magnolias," she said. "You don't see them here very often. I didn't even know florists would deliver them."

"They're something special to you?"

She nodded.

"Don't worry. I won't pry. I'm just glad he's done well."

She nodded happily. "He's done very well. Very well indeed."

"So much so that you can forgive him for sending cut flowers?"

She chuckled. "Yeah. I might have been a little ungracious about that last time. I do prefer to leave things alone so they can live, but these are lovely, and it's such a nice gesture."

"I'm starting to feel a little inadequate here. I should send Piper flowers." He looked a little shamefaced. "I used to send the red roses all the time."

"Yeah, when they were a thank you for a good time. You're right. You should send some to your fiancée, just to let her know you love her."

Cam gave her a sly smile. "You mean like Antonio did with you?"

She felt the heat in her cheeks. She might be coming around to the idea that they were falling in love, but it still felt strange to admit to Cam so soon. She nodded slightly. "Anyway. I should get back to work, and so should you." She took the flowers back to her office. Cam might tease, but she wanted to read the note alone.

She set the flowers down on her desk and opened the little envelope. Her eyes welled with tears and a lump formed in her throat when she read the card.

I love you.

A xx

Her cell phone rang, bringing her back to her senses.

"Hey, Chelsea. How are you?"

"I'm great, but I'm home alone this week. Grant's out of town. Do you want to come over for dinner?"

"I can't tonight."

Chelsea laughed. "You're not going to turn into that girl on me, are you? The one who dumps her friends when she meets a new man."

"No. You know me better than that, but we already made plans for this evening. How about tomorrow?"

"I can't. Wednesday?"

"That works."

"Great. Do you want to come to the cottage?"

Mary Ellen laughed. "What, are you going to cook for me?"

Chelsea laughed with her. "Err, no. I was thinking you could pick up some Chinese food on the way over."

"That's more like it. Okay. It sounds like a plan to me. I have to run for now. I'll call you when I finish work on Wednesday."

"You're going to make me wait until then?"

Mary Ellen smirked. She'd wondered if she was going to get away so easily. "Wait for what?"

"You know what! I want to hear all about your weekend."

"It was amazing, Chels. I have to make you wait until then because I'm going to need to bend your ear for hours, and I don't have hours to spare right now."

"You're not helping. You're just making me more impatient to hear what's going on. But I can wait—as long as you're happy. Are you happy?"

Mary Ellen grinned. "I'm happy. In fact, this may be the happiest I've ever been."

"That's awesome! I'm so happy for you. Okay. Wednesday. And in the meantime, have fun."

"Thanks. I will."

She set her phone down and then picked it up again. She was going to Antonio's tonight—after she'd been back to her apartment for more clothes and toiletries, but it was only polite to call and thank him for the flowers. She dialed his number and listened to it ring. Perhaps he was busy. It was the middle of the work day, after all. She hadn't called him at work before.

"Hey, bella," he answered. She loved the way he called her that.

"Hey. I just wanted to say thank you for the flowers."

"You're welcome. They took some finding."

She laughed. "I'll bet they did, and to get them here so quickly."

He chuckled. "It took some doing, but as long as you like them."

"I love them. Thank you."

"I should send you some every day."

Mary Ellen frowned. She loved the flowers, but she hated the thought of them being cut for her when they could bloom for months on the tree. "You don't need to do that."

"You don't want more?" He sounded disappointed.

"Don't get me wrong. I love them, but I'd rather they lived on, on the tree."

He was quiet for a moment. "Okay, no more to be cut for you. What time are you coming tonight?"

"I don't know. I probably won't get done here until six and then I need to go home and get my things. What time will you be home? How's your day going?"

He sighed. "It's a busy one, for sure, but I can be home by six-thirty."

"I'll tell you what, why don't you call me when you get home? That way you can stay at work as long as you need to, and I'll just come over when you're back."

He was silent for so long she wondered if they'd been cut off. "No," he said eventually.

"No?"

He laughed. "I have a better idea. I'll try to be home before you get there, but don't wait for me. When you're ready, just go on over to the house."

She wasn't sure what she thought of that.

"There's a key hanging behind the light by the door. You can let yourself in. Make yourself at home."

She still didn't say anything.

"I'd love to think you'd be there when I get home."

She couldn't help but smile at that. "I'll see what time I'm ready. Okay?"

She could hear the smile in his voice. "Okay. Ciao, bella."

At six-thirty she stood in the middle of her living room and looked at the bag she'd packed. She couldn't decide what to do. She could pick up the bag and do as Antonio had said—head over to his house and wait for him to get home—or she could wait around here for him to call and say he was back. It wasn't such a big decision in any practical way. But it wasn't about the practical. If she went over there by herself and let herself in, and she was there waiting for him when he came home from work, that would be taking their relationship a step further. She sat down on the sofa and sighed. Not going would mean that she wasn't ready to take that step. She thought back to her conversation with Cam earlier. If she thought it was inevitable that she and Antonio would end up together, what was the point in taking her time? She smiled and got to her feet. If this was going to be a whirlwind ride, she may as well put herself in the center of it. There was no point trying to hold back and take things slowly. She picked up her bag and closed up the apartment. Maybe she'd pick up something to eat on the way over.

~ ~ ~

Antonio grinned when he got home and saw Mary Ellen's car parked in the driveway. He hadn't expected her to come. The fact that she had gave him hope that she was ready to move things forward more quickly than he'd thought.

He parked in the garage and ran up the steps that led into the mudroom off the kitchen. His chest buzzed with happiness when he opened the door and she was there at the sink, rinsing dishes. This was what he wanted. This was how he wanted his life to be—to come home from work and find her waiting for him.

She spun around at the sound of the door opening. "Damn, you scared me."

He went to her and wrapped his arms around her. "No need to be scared, my love. It's only me." He planted a kiss on top of her head. "I'm glad you came."

She smiled up at him. "I am, too. I almost didn't, but …" she shrugged.

She might not want to say it, but he knew what she meant. She'd made a decision, and it was one he was going to do his best to make sure she wouldn't regret.

Chapter Sixteen

Antonio was glad it was Friday. Mary Ellen had stayed with him all week—even on Wednesday when she'd gone out for dinner with Chelsea. His week at work had been less enjoyable. He'd spent most of his time putting out fires and fielding calls from customers who were concerned about the Sicilian wines. He'd talked to Marcos a couple of times, but each time, he'd claimed to be busy and that he'd call back. Antonio was starting to get worried. He'd set aside an hour this morning to get hold of him and figure out what was going on.

He picked up his phone and then set it down again. He couldn't imagine what his brother was going through. He felt bad for him. He needed to remember that when they talked and not just get mad at him about how he was letting things slide with the business. He stared out the window for a few moments, thinking about Marcos. He was more serious than Antonio. More driven—at least until now. He wasn't used to failing at anything, and although his marriage hadn't been a happy one, Antonio knew that he was taking the divorce hard.

He blew out a sigh and picked up the phone again. Instead of calling Marcos, he dialed his parents' number.

"Pronto."

"Pronto."

"Antonio! It's good to hear your voice, son. How are you?"

"I'm doing well, Dad. Very well. I'll tell you about it soon. How are you and Mom?"

"We're fine." He didn't sound fine.

"Really? What's going on?"

"We're worried about your brother."

"Yeah. I am, too. What's happening with him?"

"Caterina is giving him a hard time. I'm so glad they never had children. I can't imagine …"

"No." Antonio didn't like Caterina. She was beautiful, but there was nothing soft about her. She was all hard edges and hard-nosed.

"Is she taking him to the cleaners?"

"No. You know how shrewd your brother is? Well, it turns out he had her sign a prenup. She's trying everything she can to get out of it; she's throwing all kinds of dirt at him. Part of me thinks it'd be easier for him to give her the money."

Antonio sighed. "It might be, but I'm sure she wouldn't be pleasant with him even then."

"That's true. It's funny; we always worried about you with the ladies. We never thought it would be Marcos who'd have to go through this kind of hell."

Antonio frowned. "What did you have to worry about with me? I didn't get married."

His dad chuckled. "No, but I always half expect to see kiss-and-tell pictures in the magazines, or hear about some woman who claims she's the mother of my grandchild."

Antonio laughed. "You should have a little more faith in me. I never got up in anything like that, and I'm not likely to now."

"Why not?"

"I've met someone, Dad."

"You have? I thought you met someone every week."

"I used to, but not anymore. This is it. She's the one."

"My goodness. Who is she?"

"You've met her. She works with Cam; she's his assistant. Mary Ellen."

The line was quiet for a moment. "The blonde?"

"Yeah."

"I see, and you think this is serious?"

"It is."

"Well, I'm sorry, but your brother's situation leaves me a little wary. Be careful, okay?"

"I will." He'd hoped for a more enthusiastic reaction to his news, but the timing wasn't great. He let it go—for now. There'd be plenty of time for him to tell them all about her, for them to get to know her. "What's happening at the winery?"

"Chaos and mayhem, by the sounds of it. Are you going to come and help smooth things over? The business could use you here, and I think your brother might appreciate your support, too."

Antonio frowned. "I could come." He sighed. "Do you think he would appreciate it, or do you think it'd seem that I'm interfering?"

His dad sighed. "I wouldn't worry about treading on his toes. He needs help—with the winery and with his personal life. He's too proud to let me do anything, or your mom. You're probably the only person who can help him through this."

"Okay. Let me get a few things in order and I'll be there."

"Thanks, son."

"Of course. Is Mom around?"

"She's out. She's at her craft group. I'll get her to call you."

"Okay. Thanks. I'm going to call Marcos and tell him I'm coming."

"Good. See you soon. Love you, son."

"Love you, too, Dad. Bye."

Antonio hung up and stared out of the window. He shook his head sadly. He felt for his brother and hoped he could help him. He wanted to be there for him, but at the same time, the timing wasn't wonderful. He wanted to be here with Mary Ellen, too. He wondered what she'd think. He hoped she'd understand, and that it wouldn't make her think he was backing off or wanting to slow things down between them. He smiled as a thought struck him. There was one way he knew he could prove to her that him leaving for a while didn't mean that he didn't want to be with her. He checked his watch. He'd call Marcos now and then get out of here. He'd need to make a stop on his way home.

~ ~ ~

Mary Ellen smiled to herself as she opened the front door and let herself in. She'd gotten used to coming home here after work. Antonio had given her the spare key that had been behind the light on Monday, and she'd come back here every night since. She turned around to take everything in as she entered the grand foyer. Could this really be her home? "Why not?" she asked out loud. It was a beautiful home, and it belonged to a beautiful man. A man who loved her. She hugged herself at the thought. He loved her. He told her every chance he got—and she loved hearing it every single time. She had a plan tonight. When he came home, she was going to tell him that she loved him. She'd told him she was falling for him, said that she could see herself loving him, but she hadn't yet come out and said, plain and simple, I love you. And she knew she did. She might have wrestled with how fast things were happening between them, but she couldn't deny that she'd fallen head over heels in love with him. He'd been her fantasy guy, and now her fantasy was a reality—only the reality beat the fantasy, hands down. Not only was he a great guy, when she'd thought him not to be, but even all her old sexual fantasies paled in comparison with the reality. The imaginary guy who'd helped her fill her nights had only been as good in bed as she could imagine. It turned out that her imagination had been sorely lacking, and the real Antonio had opened up a whole new world in the bedroom.

She went through to the kitchen and put her purse down on the counter. He'd said he was going to cook for her tonight—the Chicken Marsala that they'd never gotten around to eating the first night she came here. She didn't know what time he'd be back, but he'd called her earlier to say that he shouldn't be too late, so not to go snacking on anything and spoil her appetite. She smiled. She didn't need to eat, but she did want her usual Friday night treat. He'd very sweetly bought everything she needed to make her Margaritas and she fixed herself one and took it out onto the terrace. She loved it out here. The view was amazing. She sat down on one of the loungers, but couldn't settle there—apparently, she wasn't totally relaxed here yet. Instead, she took her drink and sat at the table. She blew out a big happy sigh and took in the view. Who would ever have thought that this would be her life? She smiled as she remembered what Antonio had said about being grateful to David. He was right. She was grateful to him now—if he hadn't dumped her she wouldn't be sitting here right now, sipping her Margarita, and waiting for her wonderful man to come home to her.

She had to wonder what her mom would make of all this. She'd only spoken to her a couple of times since that night at Molly's. She wasn't angry at her, but her feelings were still a little hurt that her mom thought she should take David back and be grateful that he wanted her again. She pulled her phone out of her pocket. She should give them a call, maybe she'd even tell them about Antonio. Though she wouldn't expect too much enthusiasm.

She set her phone down on the table when she heard the garage door open. He was home. She could call her parents another time. Right now, she had to go tell a certain Sicilian that she loved him.

She met him in the kitchen and he came and closed his arms around her. There was a gleam in his eyes that made her wonder what he was up to.

"Hey, bella. I love coming home to find you here."

"I love being here."

"You do?" The way he smiled made her more curious as to what he had up his sleeve.

"I do. I love being with you."

He smiled and planted a kiss on her lips.

She decided she might as well go for it. There was no point waiting. "I love being with you because I love you."

He cupped her face between his hands and kissed her. Then he lifted his head and looked into her eyes. "You do? You're sure?"

She laughed. "I'm sure. I wouldn't tell you if I didn't know for certain."

He kissed her again and wrapped her in a big hug before holding her at arm's-length. "You just made me the happiest man in the world. I love you, Mary Ellen. I love you and I always will. I'm a lucky man."

She put her hands on his shoulders and reached up to kiss him. "And I'm a lucky lady."

~ ~ ~

After they'd eaten, Antonio led her out onto the terrace and sat her down at the table. "Wait here. I'll be right back."

She gave him a puzzled look, but did as he asked.

He hurried back into the kitchen to fetch the Tiramisu and the items he'd picked up after work. He opened the fridge and then closed it again. Was it tempting fate? No. He opened it again and took out a bottle of champagne. He had to believe they'd be celebrating after dessert.

She laughed when he came back out. "You should have let me help out."

He shrugged as he set out the desserts and the champagne, the flutes, and the most important thing—his little bag of goodies. She raised an eyebrow at him. "What's that?"

"Tiramisu." He tried to look innocent, but she wasn't going for it.

"I know that. I mean, what's in the bag?"

"A surprise."

She made a face at him.

"Oh, that's right. You don't like surprises." He picked up the bag. He'd wanted to wait until after dessert, but he was too impatient anyway. He fished inside it and pulled out his first gift. He handed it over with a smile. "I thought you might want this."

She took it from him with a puzzled look. "It's a garage opener?"

He nodded. "You shouldn't have to leave your car in the driveway."

She laughed. "It's hardly in any danger out there. Even if someone tried to take it, they wouldn't get out of the gate."

He shook his head. She was missing the point. "It's not about someone taking your car; it's about you keeping your car here."

"Okay." She still looked puzzled. "Thanks."

"When you come home before I do, you can go straight into the garage."

She nodded again, missing his point about this being home.

He needed to do better. He pulled out the key he'd had cut and handed it over. "This is for you, too, if you want it."

She took it with the same puzzled look on her face. "Thanks, do you need the other one back as the spare?"

He let out a frustrated chuckle. "No. The point is that that one was the spare. I don't want you to have the spare. I want you to have your very own key, and your own garage opener so you can come and go as you please. You should be able to do that—if you live here."

"But I don't … oh!" She met his gaze. "Are you saying …?"

He laughed and took hold of her hands. "Apparently, I'm not doing a very good job of it, but yes, I'm asking you to move in with me."

She nodded slowly, and he held his breath, not sure if that meant yes or if she was thinking it over.

He tried to wait for her to answer, but he couldn't. "Do you want to?"

She met his gaze and nodded again. "Yes. I do."

He grinned and lifted her hands to his lips. "Thank you. You just made me an even happier man."

She was smiling, but she didn't say anything.

"Are you sure?"

She nodded happily. "Sorry; yes, I am. I'm thrilled. I'm just taking a moment to get used to the idea—and to get past my need for things to go more slowly. I want it just as much as you do, so why waste time?"

Antonio grinned. "I love it when you think like that."

She laughed. "So do I. So far."

~ ~ ~

"Do you want to go out for breakfast?"

Mary Ellen looked at him. Did she? She wasn't sure.

He narrowed his eyes at her. "Are you ashamed to be seen out with me?"

She laughed. "No. It's not that, though I take it that means you want to go to Molly's?"

"She does serve the best breakfast in town."

"She does." Mary Ellen got to her feet. "Yeah, let's do it. I'm sure it won't be a surprise to anyone to see us having breakfast together."

He chuckled. "So you were ashamed of me?"

"No!" she pushed at his arm. "I'm sure no girl has ever been ashamed of you. All I was hesitating over was if I'm ready to tell people that I'm moving in with you."

"You don't have to tell them if you don't want to."

She shook her head at him. "I know that much, but I also know you well enough to know that you're bound to let it slip out."

He gave her a shamefaced grin. "You do know me well. I want to tell the world."

She smiled. "And I said yes, let's go. So apparently, I do, too."

He held the door open for her when they got to Molly's and she stopped dead just inside the door, making him walk into the back of her. He slid his arms around her waist and rested his head on her shoulder. "Problem?"

She sighed. "No problem, but look. At least we won't need to repeat our news over and over to everyone. The whole gang's here." She nodded toward a large table in the back where all the Hamiltons were sitting. Mr. and Mrs. Hamilton had joined their children and their partners and even Gene and his wife Rita were there.

Antonio kissed her cheek and took hold of her hand. "We don't have to join them."

"Too late," she replied as Cameron waved and got to his feet. Mrs. Hamilton met her gaze with a smile and beckoned them over.

"It's good to see the two of you." Mr. Hamilton gave her a knowing smile then nodded at Antonio.

"You will join us, won't you?"

Antonio raised an eyebrow at her and she nodded. How could they refuse?

Cam caught her eye. "Sorry I didn't invite you. It's just that we have some news we wanted to share with the family."

Antonio gave him a hurt look. "I'm not family anymore?"

Mr. Hamilton gave his nephew a stern look. "Of course you are. We were being considerate of your situation." He winked at Mary Ellen and she couldn't help smiling back at him. He seemed so formal, yet he was so warm and kind.

Cameron punched his arm. "Don't, okay. Piper and I have decided to change our wedding plans. We'll both be more comfortable with a smaller celebration and we wanted to tell Mom and Dad first."

Mary Ellen smiled at Piper. "That's good, you should do whatever works best for you."

Piper looked uncomfortable, but Mrs. Hamilton put a hand on her arm. "She's right. You're the most important one in all of this. We're just happy to be invited to whatever the two of you want to do."

Mr. Hamilton nodded his agreement. "That's right, and I believe you were about to tell us what your new plans are?"

Cam grinned around at everyone. "I don't know what you're going to make of this, but we've decided we want to have just a small ceremony and reception in ..." He looked around again, drawing out the moment."

"Tell us already!" said Chelsea impatiently.

Piper laughed. "In Summer Lake."

"Thank God for that!" said Chelsea. "For one horrible moment I thought you were about to say Vegas."

They all laughed at that.

"No, that's not my style at all," said Piper. "It's okay for the parties, but not for our wedding."

Mr. Hamilton chuckled. "If it weren't for parties in Vegas the two of you might never have gotten together."

Mary Ellen loved the way Cam and Piper smiled at each other. She hoped that someday she and Antonio would have memories that made them smile like that.

"What will happen with all the arrangements you made?" asked Antonio.

She looked at him. He couldn't know what she'd gone through canceling all of her own wedding arrangements all those years ago. It surprised her that the thought even occurred to him.

Cam smiled. "I'll take care of it all on Monday."

Mary Ellen smiled. Of course he would. Piper wouldn't have to go through what she had—even if it was under much happier circumstances, no bride should have to cancel her wedding arrangements.

"And what about you? Have you made any plans yet?"

Mary Ellen's heart jumped into her throat as Gene smiled at her. How did he know that her getting married was even a possibility? He smirked at her and a wave of relief rushed through her as he turned to look at Chelsea.

"We haven't decided yet, have we?" She smiled up at Grant.

He laughed. "I'm just waiting to hear what you want, and we'll do it."

Mr. Hamilton smiled at him. "Just don't agree to anything too crazy?"

Grant shrugged his shoulders. "I'll try, but I can't make any promises."

Chelsea made a face at her dad. "You can make all the noises you like. If I want to get married while skydiving, you'll be there."

They all laughed as Mr. Hamilton nodded sadly. "I will. I will."

The server came to take their orders and they caught up with each other's news while they ate. Afterward, everyone went their separate ways with promises to catch up soon. Mary Ellen felt a little deflated as they walked back to the car. She'd been expecting to hear everyone's reaction to her moving in with Antonio, but it hadn't been the time or the place to talk about it. Everyone had enough going on in their own lives.

When Antonio reached the car, he held the door open for her and pecked her lips before she got in. "Is everything okay?"

She nodded.

"I'm disappointed, too, but we'll tell them when we see them next."

Chapter Seventeen

They spent the rest of the day hanging out at the house. Antonio didn't usually spend much time at home, but with Mary Ellen there, there was no place else he'd rather be. She'd set herself up on one of the loungers out on the terrace. She looked so at home reading her book, and that was what he wanted her to be—at home, here with him.

Her phone rang, and she reached for it, but then looked up at him. "It must be yours. It's not mine."

It made him smile that they both had the same ringtone, though it did get a little confusing sometimes. He went to fetch his from the counter. It was Muse.

"Hello?"

"Antonio. I'm sorry to disturb you." It was Rodney. "I've found something of a discrepancy in the accounts. I think I know what's happening, but I don't want to act on my intuition until I know that you agree."

Antonio frowned. "You think someone's stealing?"

"I'm afraid so."

Antonio blew out a sigh. "Are you there now?"

"Yes, but it can wait. I know this is your weekend."

"It's okay, hold on a minute." He looked at Mary Ellen. He hated to leave her, but employee theft wasn't something to take lightly. He couldn't just let it ride, and it wasn't right to offload all the responsibility onto Rodney.

She looked up. "Is everything all right?"

"No. There's a problem at Muse. Would you mind if I run over there and sort it out?"

"Of course not. Go. Do what you need to do. I'm fine here."

"Thanks." He lifted his phone back to his ear. "I'll be right over Rodney."

When he got to the wine bar and Rodney showed him the receipts and the takings, it was all too obvious that the new guy on the upstairs bar had been taking home more than tips. Antonio nodded sadly. He liked to give people a chance, to believe the best of people, but unfortunately, in this case there was no room for doubt. "What time's he due in for his shift?"

Rodney checked his watch. "He should be here in twenty minutes."

"Okay. I'll wait and take care of it myself."

"Thank you." Rodney smile awkwardly. "I can do it if you want me to, but I do find firing people rather distasteful."

Antonio laughed and grasped his shoulder. "I'm sure you do. Don't worry. I wouldn't ask you to. You're here to enhance the finer side, not to get your hands dirty with the darker side of the business."

Rodney smiled. "Can I get you anything while you wait?"

Antonio shook his head. "I'm fine, thanks. I'm making a special dinner tonight."

"Are things going well?"

Antonio grinned. "That's an understatement. I asked her to move in with me, and she said yes." He couldn't help it, he had to share his news with someone.

Unfortunately, Rodney didn't seem thrilled to hear it.

"You're not happy for me?"

"Of course, I am. I suppose I'm a little more cautious than you. Are you sure about her?"

"I couldn't be surer, Rodney. I'm in love with her."

"And does she feel the same? Are you sure of her intentions?"

Antonio laughed. "My intentions are honorable, if that's what you mean."

"No. It isn't. Is she in love with you? I'm sorry, perhaps it's this little incident that's making me lose trust in human nature. But you must admit, you're quite a prize."

Antonio frowned. "She's not after me for my money, if that's what you mean. She loves me. She's more cautious about this than I am. It's me that's rushing things along, not her."

Rodney nodded. "I'm sorry. I didn't mean to offend. I'm only looking out for you."

Antonio wrapped his arm around the older man's shoulders and hugged him into his side. "I know, and I appreciate it, but you don't have to worry about Mary Ellen. She's as genuine as they come. She's the real deal, and she and I—we're meant to be. I'm not going to make the same mistake my brother made."

"How is Marcos?"

"Not good." That reminded Antonio that he was supposed to call him.

"I'm sorry to hear that. Give him my best when you speak to him. I hope we'll see him back here soon."

"Will do. In fact, I'm going to give him a quick call while I wait."

~ ~ ~

Mary Ellen paced the living room and looked at her watch. When Antonio left he'd said he shouldn't be more than an hour. He'd already been gone for nearly three. She'd been fine for a while, but now she was getting antsy. This was supposedly her first full day living here and he'd just disappeared. If this was a sign of how he thought their life should be, she wasn't sure she was interested. She took a deep breath to calm herself. That was ridiculous! She knew all about having to go into work on the weekend, and about work problems eating up far more time than you expected them to. He'd gone into work, that was all. The nagging little voice insisted on reminding her that his work also happened to be his playground—the place where he met women and took them home to bed.

She let out a frustrated laugh. She was being stupid, and she knew it. It was just a little doubt creeping in and she needed to kick it to the curb before it could take a hold. The poor guy was probably stressed out over some issue at work, and the last thing he needed was to come home and find her doubting him.

She smiled as she heard the garage door open and went to meet him in the kitchen. He looked stressed. She went to him and closed her arms around him. "Hey. I missed you."

"I'm sorry." He kissed the top of her head and stepped away from her.

Something was wrong. She knew it. "What is it? Is something wrong at Muse?"

He shook his head sadly. "Muse is fine, it was just a little problem. It's sorted; I fired him. It's not that. It's Marcos."

"Your brother?"

"Yeah. You know things haven't been great with him? Well, they're getting worse. I called him while I was waiting." He shook his head. "He's in a bad way. He was drunk. Which isn't like him. He says he can't do it. He can't run the winery. Caterina's pushed him to his limits." He came to her and took hold of her hands. "He asked me to go, to be there with him."

Mary Ellen nodded.

"Do you mind?"

"Don't be silly. Of course I don't. He's your brother, you should be there for him."

"I know, but the timing. You just moved in, and I don't know how long it'll take, and …" He shook his head sadly.

"It's okay. It doesn't matter. Life does this, it messes up plans when we make them. We'll be fine. When are you leaving? I can go home."

"No!" He looked horrified. "This is your home."

She touched his cheek. "It isn't yet, though, is it? I'd like it to be, and when you come back, we can try this again. But I don't want to stay here if you're not here. I didn't sign up to be with your house. I signed up to be with you."

"Then come with me?" He looked so hopeful, but it wasn't realistic.

She shook her head. "For one thing, you're going there to spend time with your brother. He needs you. And for another, I have to work."

He closed his arms around her and blew out a sigh. "You're right. I'm sorry. Please, will you stay here?"

"I don't want to. It wouldn't feel right. I'd rather go back to my apartment for now. When you come back, so will I."

He leaned back to look into her eyes. "Do you promise?"

She nodded. For some reason, she didn't want to make that promise. Things might change while he was gone—or was that just the stupid doubts taking hold again? It was. She smiled and planted a kiss on his lips. "I promise."

"Thank you." He hugged her close and she relaxed against him.

"When will you leave?"

"Tomorrow, if I can. I need to book a flight."

She nodded. "Why don't you get onto that and I'll go get us something for dinner?"

"No. I was going to cook for you. If this is going to be our last night together, it should be special."

"It will be." She nodded, understanding it herself as she said it. "This is our first real chance to work together as a team. To join forces in the face of life throwing us a curveball. We can do this. You take care of whatever you need to do. I'll go get us something to eat, and then later, after you're packed, we can relax and hang out and enjoy each other's company. It won't work if you expect me to sit around while you have things to do and then sit around again while you cook for me. We want to be a team, don't we?"

He smiled down at her and shook his head.

"You don't want us to be a team?"

He shook his head again and landed a kiss on her lips. "I want us to be a couple."

~ ~ ~

The next morning, Antonio woke early. He hadn't been able to get a direct flight to Rome. He'd have to fly out of San Francisco at two to get to Chicago. The family jet would pick him up from Rome on Monday morning. He sighed. He'd need to leave here by nine.

Mary Ellen turned over and smiled at him. "Good morning."

He dropped a kiss on her lips. There was nothing good about it as far as he was concerned. He didn't want to leave her. He wanted his brother to be okay. He closed his arms around her and hugged her to his chest. "Say you'll stay here?"

She shook her head. "I'm sorry, but I don't want to. It doesn't feel right."

"Okay." He didn't want to push her and make her uncomfortable. "Will you pop in sometimes and keep an eye on the place for me?"

"Of course."

"Thanks."

"Do you want me to make us some breakfast? You're going to have to get up and get on the road soon."

"I don't need breakfast. I'd rather spend the time right here with you."

She smiled and nuzzled her face into his neck. "I was hoping you might say that."

He chuckled. "Only because you don't want to cook."

"Nope. It's not because I don't want to cook; it's because I want to do something that rhymes with it."

He rolled her onto her back. "And what might that be?"

"I think you know."

"Mm-hmm. I think I do, but I want to hear you say it."

"I want you to fuck me."

His body came to life hearing her say it, but he shook his head. "Much as I'd like to, I have something else in mind." He cupped her breast and loved the way she sighed.

"I'll beg if you want me to."

"I don't." He trailed his hand down over her stomach and slid it between her legs. She gasped as he began to stroke her. She was already hot and wet for him.

"What is it that you have in mind?" she asked as she began to rock her hips in time with his hand.

"I want to make love to you."

"Oh." She sighed as he positioned himself on top of her, spreading her legs wide to receive him.

His cock throbbed, eager to be inside her, but he moved slowly, resting at her entrance as he watched her face. Her hands came up around his ass, urging him on. But still, he moved slowly, pushing inside her an inch at a time, until he couldn't resist, and he thrust hard, making them both moan. This time was different. He kissed her as their bodies moved together. She held his face between her hands as she lifted her hips to meet each thrust. It was a slow burn, long drawn out exquisite torture as he brought them both to the edge of orgasm, then backed off the pace, wanting to make it last. He could feel the beads of sweat on his shoulders and see them in her hairline as they drove each other crazy. She tightened around him as he pulsated inside her. The tension was building so hard, but he wanted to make this last. He wanted her to feel and to know that this was love.

She tensed and clenched around him. "Antonio!" she gasped as her orgasm took her.

It took him too, the fire in his belly tore through him in a heat-wave that ignited every cell of his body. They moved together frantically, their bodies becoming one. He never wanted the moment to end, but of course, it did. Eventually they lay spent in each other's arms. He rolled off her and hugged her to him, peppering the top of her head with kisses.

"I love you, Antonio."

His eyes filled with tears hearing her say it. "I love you, Mary Ellen. This is just the beginning."

Chapter Eighteen

"Cheer up," said Chelsea. "You should be happy that you get a night out with the girls. That overbearing Italian cousin of mine has been hogging you since you started dating him."

Mary Ellen made a face. "Sorry. You know I'm happy to be here."

"You could have fooled me," said Molly as she set a Margarita down in front of her and a Cosmo in front of Chelsea. "You look lost and lonely, and believe me, I know how you feel."

Mary Ellen raised her glass to her. "Cheers."

Chelsea shook her head. "It's not like you, Molly. Don't go thinking that. Antonio's been gone a week. From what he's told Mary Ellen and Grant, he'll be back by next weekend. It's not like he's moving back there."

Molly nodded. "I know. Sorry."

"I don't get it," said Mary Ellen. "Why would you think he's moving back there—and why would it matter to you?"

Molly blew out a sigh. "I have to get back to the kitchen."

Chelsea raised an eyebrow at her. "Can I tell her?"

"Sure, why not. It's no secret."

"What isn't?" asked Mary Ellen, as she watched Molly walk away. "She seems upset about something."

"That's because she is. Still. After all this time."

"Still what? Give me a clue here. Why would she think that Antonio would go back to Sicily for good?"

"Because that's what Marcos did."

"So?"

"So, Molly and Marcos were like the golden couple in high school. He was a year ahead of her, and even when he went to college, they kept seeing each other. Right until he graduated." Chelsea shook her head. "At that point, instead of him coming back to run the winery here, he went back to Sicily."

"Wow! I had no idea. She didn't want to go with him?"

"She had this place. Her dad started this place when she was little, and he named it after her. It was always her destiny." Chelsea shook her head. "She didn't bother going to college, even though she could have, because she always knew she was going to run Molly's."

"Did Marcos have to go, or did he choose to?"

Chelsea shrugged. "That's the million-dollar question. Everyone thought he was going to take over Di Giovanni's here. They had a general manager, but everyone expected Marcos would take over as soon as he could."

"Was Antonio supposed to go to Sicily then?"

Chelsea chuckled. "No one ever knew what to expect of him. It turned out that with Marcos gone, he stepped up and took over the winery here. And it's never looked back since."

Mary Ellen smiled, happy to think that he'd stepped up for his family and that he hadn't just been a stand-in but had made a great success of the label. Her smile faded as she thought about Marcos and Molly. "How do you think she feels now, knowing that he's getting divorced and having such a hard time?"

"I have no idea. I keep trying to get her to talk to me, but she won't open up."

"I hope she's okay."

"She will be. She's a tough one is our Molly."

Mary Ellen nodded and watched Molly. She was smiling and laughing, bantering with customers as she took their orders, but now that she knew her story, Mary Ellen thought she could see sadness lurking behind the smile.

Her phone rang, and she fished it out of her purse. Chelsea snatched it out of her hands. "If that's Antonio, you can tell him you'll call him back later. This is girls' night."

Mary Ellen laughed and grabbed it back. "Oh, it's my mom."

"You'd better take it, then." Chelsea looked serious. "But don't let her upset you. Remember, whatever she says, she's only looking out for you in her own way."

Mary Ellen gave her a grateful smile as she answered. It was good advice. "Hi, Mom. How are you?"

"Hello, Mary Ellen. Are you busy this weekend?"

"Not particularly, why?" Mary Ellen frowned, wondering what was coming.

"I don't want to worry you, but your dad isn't doing so well. I wondered if you might want to come home and cheer him up."

"What's wrong?"

"Don't worry. Nothing's the matter with him; he's just been a bit down in the dumps lately and I know a visit from you would cheer him up. We haven't seen you since Christmas and … never mind. I shouldn't have said anything. I'm sure you're too busy."

"I'll be there. I'll let you know when I can book a flight."

"Wonderful. We'll look forward to it. See you soon, then. Bye." She hung up, leaving Mary Ellen staring at her phone.

"Is everything okay?" asked Chelsea.

Mary Ellen shook her head. "I don't know. Either my dad's ill and she doesn't want to tell me, or she's guilt-tripping me because I haven't been home in a while."

"What are you going to do?"

"Book a flight." Mary Ellen was already searching on her phone.

"Maybe Piper can take you?"

"I don't want to screw up their weekend. I'm sure they've got enough going on. They might even be going to Summer Lake to work on their wedding plans."

"There's only one way to find out." Chelsea pulled her phone out, but Mary Ellen held up a hand. "Don't. I'll maybe ask, if I can't find a flight, but I'd rather not. Let me see what I can do first."

~ ~ ~

Antonio leaned on the stone balustrade and watched the moonlight shimmer on the sea below. The night air was warm and heavy with the scent of his mom's flowers. It carried the sound of crickets and of waves crashing down below. It wrapped him in a sense of home. He'd missed it here. It had been a long week, but he and Marcos had accomplished a lot in the time he'd been here. It was Friday night and part of him wanted to rush straight back to California—to Mary Ellen, but his family was important to him, too. He was staying for the weekend to spend time with them. They'd had a wonderful family dinner this evening and he'd come out here to enjoy the night air after his parents had gone to bed.

"Mind if I join you?"

"I was hoping you might." He smiled at his brother.

"It's been quite a week, no?"

"You can say that again."

"I'm sorry I dragged you over here, but I couldn't do it by myself."

"I'm glad you asked me. Glad I could help."

"But now you want to go home, right?"

Antonio smiled. "Honestly, this place is just as much my home as over there. It's not California I'm in a rush to get back to."

Marcos smiled. "I know. It's Mary Ellen."

"I can't wait for you to meet her. In fact, why don't you come with me?"

Marcos shook his head. "Not yet. It's too soon for me. I didn't do all this work this week to free me up, just so I can go to the other wine country. I'm going to take off for a while. You really think things will be all right here?"

Antonio punched his arm. "They'll be better than they were."

"I know. I screwed up. I let myself go under and almost took the business with me. It's not like me."

"It isn't, but it just goes to show how much you've been dealing with. Now it's all behind you. Caterina has her settlement and she'll leave you alone. Pietro can deal with everything here. He's been with us all his life. I think this promotion is exactly what he wanted, but didn't believe could ever happen. I can help him with anything he needs from over there."

Marcos blew out a big sigh. "I don't feel so wonderful knowing that I created this whole big mess, personally and professionally. I ran things down over a matter of years, and my little brother comes in and makes everything right in the space of a week."

Antonio grasped his shoulder. "It's like anything—it's easy to see solutions from the outside, and easier to implement them too."

"You mean it's easier to fix something when you weren't the one who screwed it up?"

"Don't be so hard on yourself. You've bailed me out enough times."

Marcos shrugged. "No need to dwell on it all, I guess. You've given me a fresh start. I'm going to make the most of it."

"Do you know where you'll go?"

"I'm going to start in Rome, then maybe Paris, London. I don't know. I want to see some city life for a while."

"Don't forget San Francisco."

He smiled. "I'll come see you when I'm ready. I need to get right with myself first."

"No pressure. Just know I'll be waiting impatiently."

Marcos laughed. "You'll forget all about me when you get back to Mary Ellen."

"You may be right there." He looked at his watch. "I might go and give her a call, tell her I'm coming home."

"You do that. Give her my best, tell her thanks for letting me borrow you and sorry about the timing."

Antonio smiled and walked away to make the call. The phone made the usual clicks and tones as it made the international connection and then he heard it ring. It only rang once and then went straight to voicemail. That was odd. He checked his watch. It was ten here, which meant it was two in the afternoon there. Maybe she was in a meeting?

He hung up and tried again. Maybe it was the connection that hadn't gone through somehow? Nope. It went straight to voicemail this time, too. "Hey, bella. I miss you. I wanted to hear your voice. I'm going to bed soon. I guess you're busy. I'll call you tomorrow. I love you." He hung up and went back into the house. That was the first time he'd missed her when he called. He didn't like it.

When he woke up in the morning, the first thing he did was check his phone. He smiled when he saw a text from her.

Sorry I missed you. I had to go home.

I'll call you when I get chance.

Love you. Oxo

He frowned and sat up in bed. Home? Did that mean she'd gone back to Ohio? Why? He tapped out a reply.

Is everything OK?

He stared at his phone for a few minutes, waiting for her reply, but it didn't come. He got up and headed for the shower, feeling uneasy. He hoped her parents were okay.

He checked his phone again as soon as he stepped out of the shower and went to sit on the bed in his towel to read her reply.

Sorry. I'm pissed! My mom made it sound like there was something up with my dad so I rushed back here. He's fine! It turns out David's here and she wanted me to see him. He fed her some bullshit about how he made a big mistake and wants me back. I've told her, and I've told him – I'm not interested! I'll call you in the morning.

Antonio scowled. He didn't want to wait. The time difference was a pain in the ass. He looked at his watch. Seven-thirty here was ten-thirty in California. But wait. She was in Ohio, that was Eastern time, so it would be one-thirty. Why was she up at one-thirty in the morning? He pressed his lips together. Was she with David? She said she'd told him she wasn't interested—so, she'd seen him. Had she been out with him?

He stared at his phone. He wanted to call her and ask what was going on, but he shook his head. This was one time when he needed to be patient. He had to wait for her to call and tell him all about it. He picked up his towel and dried himself off. He had to keep pushing away thoughts that she was with David. It was crazy; it was just jealousy and there was no reason for it. She'd told him about it. It wasn't like she was trying to hide anything from him.

He got dressed and ran downstairs. He was going to have to do something to occupy himself. He'd drive himself nuts otherwise.

His mom was in the kitchen pouring coffee. "Ciao, bello. You want some?"

He nodded and went to kiss her cheek. "Please."

She gave him a puzzled look. "Did you get out of the wrong side of the bed?"

He shrugged. "No. I'm good."

"You're not. Want to tell your mama?"

He chuckled. "I'm a not a little kid anymore."

She reached up and kissed his cheek and set a mug of coffee in front of him. "I know this, but you'll always be my baby." He sat down, and she ruffled his hair, making him chuckle.

"Did you not get a chance to speak to your lady? Is that why you're grumpy?"

He nodded. "Yeah. I missed her last night and this morning I found out why. She had to go home to Ohio and her ex-fiancé is there—trying to get her back."

His mom frowned. "That's an asshole move!"

He had to laugh. She didn't pull any punches. "Exactly."

"So, are you going to leave us and go claim her?"

He pursed his lips and met her gaze.

"You should. This asshole might not be her fiancé anymore, but neither are you."

Antonio swallowed. "Not formally, no, but …"

His mom wagged her finger at him. "But nothing. You haven't made it official. She's free until you … until, how do they say?" She chuckled. "You have to put a ring on it!"

Antonio had to laugh. "I intend to, but it's too soon."

"The road to hell is paved with good intentions, Antonio. This isn't like you. You don't talk about it. You do it. Do it now."

He blew out a sigh. "I want to! I was trying to be patient."

His mom gave him a stern look. "Patience doesn't suit you, and it doesn't seem to be working out for you, does it? You just have to hope this other man isn't going to steal her away from you."

"He won't. She doesn't want him; she loves me. I know she does, and I love her."

His mom threw her hands in the air. "Then why is it too soon to get married? Go to her, ask her, marry her, before it's too late."

He stared at her for a few moments. "I'd have your blessing?"

"Of course! And your father's. We've both been expecting you to tell us about your wedding plans. We know, we can see, this is it for you. This Mary Ellen, she's the one."

"She is."

"So, go make her your wife, but don't you dare get married without us there. We only need forty-eight hours' notice, so you have no excuses, carino."

He got his feet. "Okay."

"You're going now?"

He nodded. "I'm going to pack, and I need to change my flights. I'm going to Ohio."

Chapter Nineteen

Mary Ellen sat in her bedroom and tried calling Antonio again. She hadn't been able to get through since she woke up this morning. It was getting late in Sicily now. His phone went to voicemail yet again. She'd already left him a message. She wasn't going to leave another one. She threw her phone down on the bed with a sigh. They hadn't spoken since she'd left California, and right now she needed him. She wanted to rant to him about what her mom had done. She still couldn't believe it. She couldn't believe David had put her up to it either. Asshole.

Apparently, he'd come to Cincinnati to interview for a job, and he'd thought he'd catch up with her folks while he was in the area.

She looked up at the sound of a knock on her bedroom door. "Come in."

Her dad poked his head around the door. "Are you okay in here, love?"

She nodded. "Yeah. Sorry. I should come down."

He stepped inside and closed the door behind him. "I'm glad to get you by yourself. I'm sorry, love. I didn't know what your mom was up to."

She smiled and patted the bed for him to sit. "I know that." Her poor dad rarely did know what her mom was scheming, and even when he found out, he didn't usually get a say in things. "I'm trying not to be mad at her. She means well in her own way."

Her dad gave her a rueful smile. "You sound like me."

She chuckled. "I'll bet you have to tell yourself something along those lines every day, don't you?"

He nodded and looked over his shoulder at the door before lowering his voice. "She does mean well, and in a way a lot of it's my fault, because I never pull her up on things. I go along with it for an easy life. But Mary El, you can't let her boss you around. You can't let her ..."

"She's not going to somehow persuade me to get back with David, if that's what you're thinking."

He blew out a big sigh of relief. "I wasn't sure. I didn't know. I know you took it hard when he ... when it ended between the two of you."

Mary Ellen took hold of his hand. "I did. I was hurt for a long time, but him dumping me was probably the best thing that's ever happened to me." She smiled as she remembered what Antonio had said. "I'm grateful to him. If we'd gotten married I would never have gone to Napa. I wouldn't have my amazing job and all my friends there. And I wouldn't have met Antonio."

Her dad frowned. "Tell me more about him? You'd said you were seeing someone new, but that's all I knew."

"Because I didn't know what to tell you. It's all happened so fast. He's amazing, Dad. I think you'll love him."

Her dad looked skeptical. "All David told us is that he's Italian and he's in the wine business. I'll be honest, love, that worries me. He sounds like a bit of a Romeo. I don't want to see you get hurt again."

Mary Ellen smiled. "Antonio would never hurt me. He loves me, Dad. I love him. This is it. He's the one."

Her dad gave her a cautious smile. "You think so?"

"I know so. He's a good man. He's a bit full of himself, but he has a heart of gold. He's honest and he's loyal. I love him, and I know he loves me." She smiled as she spoke. She knew all of it was true. She had no doubts left, only confidence in Antonio and in their future together.

"And can he support you? What does he do in the wine business? He's not in sales, is he?"

She had to laugh. "He kind of is. He's in every aspect of the business. He's the CEO of Di Giovanni Wines; his family owns it."

"Oh! So, he can take care of you, then."

She laughed. "Yes, in a style I will quite happily become accustomed to. Even though I think I do a damned good job of taking care of myself."

"You do, love. I don't mean that. I just had visions of some guy who'd mooch off you—take advantage."

"No. You've got no worries there."

They both looked up as the door opened and her mom stood there looking suspicious. "What are the two of you up to?"

Mary Ellen smiled at her. She really did think she was trying to help, but she needed to be set straight. "I'm just telling Dad about Antonio. I think you're both going to love him."

Her mom pursed her lips. "I don't like the sound of him. I don't know why you had to be so rude to David last night. I've asked if he wants to come for dinner this evening."

Mary Ellen scowled. "Well, if he's coming, I'll be going out."

"And I'll be going with her," said her dad.

Mary Ellen squeezed his hand. He wasn't going along with things for a quiet life this time. She was thrilled that he was willing to stand by her on this.

Her mom glowered at them, and then sniffed. Uh-oh. Mary Ellen knew what was coming next—martyrdom and guilt trips. "I don't know why you both treat me like this. I'm doing my very best to see you settled and happy."

Mary Ellen got to her feet and wrapped an arm around her shoulders. "I know, but you're not listening to me. I've told you and told you that I don't want to get back with David. That I'm worth more than that."

Her mom sniffed again and looked up into her eyes. "He has a good job, he's responsible. He comes from a good family."

"And he's not a good person. He's out for himself. He never cared about me, only about how I could help his career. The only reason he's interested in me now is because he thinks I could be useful to him again. See, what you don't understand, Mom, is that I have a much better job than he does. I know you think I'm just Cameron's secretary, but being his assistant isn't like being a secretary. I'm second in command of one of the biggest wine growers and distributors in the country. I have a lot of clout." She winked at her dad who was smiling proudly. He understood.

"That's all very well," said her mom. "But you're not getting any younger. You should be getting married and settling down—starting a family. David comes from a good family."

Mary Ellen smiled. "That's why I want you to listen to me about Antonio."

"Some Italian?" she asked indignantly. "You can't seriously think …"

Mary Ellen blew out a sigh and stepped away from her. She wasn't going to lose her temper with her, but she didn't want to hug her while she was talking like that.

"Don't. Don't go down that road. Listen. It's important to you that I should marry into a good family? The Di Giovannis fit the bill, okay? They're an old Sicilian family who own wineries here and in Italy. They own vast estates, private planes, and a very large business."

Her mom's eyes widened. "And why didn't you tell us this before?"

"Because you weren't interested in hearing about him. I wanted you to care about who he is, not what he has. I wanted you to meet him and like him just for himself."

"So, why haven't you brought him here?"

She didn't want to admit just how little time she and Antonio had been seeing each other. "Because we've both been so busy with work."

"And why didn't he come with you this weekend?"

"Because he had to go to Sicily to help out with the business there."

Her phone rang, and her dad picked it up and looked at the display. "It's Antonio," he said with a smile.

"Aren't you going to answer?" asked her mom.

Mary Ellen took the phone from her dad. She'd rather not have to catch Antonio up on everything with the two of them here watching her, but she couldn't wait to hear his voice.

"Hey."

"Hey, bella. How are you? Is everything all right?"

"Yeah. I'm fine. Sorry we kept missing each other. Are you okay? How are things there?"

He chuckled. "Things here are just fine. At least they will be as soon as I can figure out how to work this GPS."

"GPS? Where are you?"

"Sitting in a rental car in the Cincinnati airport."

"What?" Her heart started to race, and her hand flew up to cover her mouth. "What are you doing here?"

"Don't be mad at me, but I got a little jealous. I didn't like you running off to Ohio to see David once I was out of the country."

She laughed. "You know that's not what happened."

"I do. I'm only joking … well, mostly. There's a little bit of truth to the jealousy part. I can't help it."

"That's okay. I kind of like it. At least I know you care."

"I care, bella. I care more than you know. I missed you. I love you. I couldn't wait any longer. Is it okay if I come straight to your house?"

"Of course, but do you even know where it is?"

"Yeah. I got the address from Chelsea."

"She gave it to you and didn't warn me?"

"She doesn't know. I told her I wanted to send flowers."

She laughed. "Sneaky."

"I prefer to think of it as smart. Anyway, I'm going to hang up, so I can program this damn machine and come to you. I should see you in, what, an hour?"

"Maybe less. Call me if you get lost?"

He laughed. "I won't. I'm on my way."

~ ~ ~

It only took forty-five minutes for him to get there. It had been one hell of a day so far. After his conversation with his mom in the kitchen this morning, he'd packed his bag and bid farewell to his family with reassurances that he planned to see them again real soon. The family jet had taken him to Rome where he'd found time to do a little shopping before his flight. He'd been lucky to get a seat in First Class on a direct flight Rome to JFK, but then he'd had to sprint to make his connection to a low-budget leisure carrier on which he'd sat cramped in cattle-class, surrounded by a family of five who were coming back from their first sight-seeing trip to New York City. He smiled. Of course, he now had new friends here in Cincinnati, if he was ever in the area again. He hoped with all his heart that he would be back—for holidays and family events. Not that he cared for the place, but this was Mary Ellen's hometown.

He parked the car on the road and looked up at the house. She wasn't joking when she said she'd grown up in suburbia. Her parents' home was a neat Cape Cod. The well-kept front yard was surrounded by a formal hedge—just like about fifty percent of the other houses on the street.

He reached into the back and rummaged in his bag. He wasn't sure if he'd be invited to stay, but he was sure about one thing. He was going to ask a very important question before he left. He took what he needed out of the bag and then sat there a moment longer smiling to himself. If anyone had told him that he would propose to the love of his life in a little suburban house in Ohio he would have laughed. He was more about grand gestures. He could have made elaborate plans, done this anywhere in the world, taken her anywhere. But this was right. It might be too soon, but it would be very down-to-earth.

He looked up as the front door opened. He'd been sitting here too long, and she'd seen him. She was coming down the path to meet him. He got out of the car and couldn't wipe the grin off his face. She was even more beautiful than he remembered. She stopped a foot away from him and smiled. "Hey."

"Hey, bella." He closed the final distance between them and closed his arms around her. Her arms came up around his neck and he kissed her. He kissed her with the hunger of a starving man, and she kissed him back with the same passion. She'd missed him, too.

"Come inside! Don't do that out there."

Antonio lifted his head. A woman, who must be Mary Ellen's mom, was standing at the front door looking out at them.

He looked down at Mary Ellen who gave him an apologetic smile. "Sorry."

"What for? I get to meet your mom." He wrapped his arm around her shoulders and led her up the path, smiling at her mom as they went. "Mrs. Greene. It's such a pleasure to finally meet you." He took hold of her hand and lifted it to his lips. Her eyes grew wide as he kissed the back of her hand. "Forgive me. I'm Antonio. Antonio Di Giovanni."

~ ~ ~

Mary Ellen had to bite her lip to stop herself from laughing. Antonio pronounced his name with a full-on Italian accent, which somehow made it sound even more impressive. Her mom didn't know what to do with herself. Her disapproving scowl had melted in the face of Antonio's charming smile as they'd walked up the path. Now he was kissing her hand and she was fanning herself with the other.

"Oh, my! Well, it's nice to meet you, too. I'm sure. Come on inside." She gestured for them to go by her and caught Mary Ellen's arm as she went. Mary Ellen couldn't have been more relieved to see her beaming smile. She nodded approvingly and that was it—Antonio's charm had won the day already.

"Bill," she called. "Antonio's here!"

Mary Ellen wanted to laugh again. She said it as though she was announcing the arrival of some long awaited special guest rather than the guy she'd been referring to as some Italian only an hour ago.

Her dad appeared in the hallway from the kitchen and smiled. Mary Ellen's heart went out to him. He looked nervous. She had a feeling that was more about what her mom might do than about meeting Antonio.

Antonio went straight to him and shook his hand warmly. "Mr. Greene. Antonio Di Giovanni. It's an honor to meet you, sir. I've looked forward to this."

Her dad smiled warmly at him. "It's good to meet you, too, son. Why don't you come on out back? I've got the grill going. I thought we could have some burgers. I don't know much about wine, but I've got some cold beers on ice."

Mary Ellen couldn't hold back a giggle at the sound of her mom's sputtering. "Bill! What are you thinking? We'll go out for dinner, somewhere nice."

To Mary Ellen's surprise and great pleasure, her dad shook his head firmly. "No, Vera. We won't. We're going to hang out here at the house and relax and get to know each other, right, Mary El?"

She nodded happily.

"That sounds good to me," said Antonio. He turned and put his arm around her mom's shoulders. "I hope you'll come to Napa to see us soon? I know a few nice restaurants there we can go to."

Mary Ellen couldn't resist. She smiled at her mom. "He's being too modest. He owns the best restaurant in town."

Her mom's eyes looked as though they might pop out of her head. "Oh! That's nice," was all she managed to sputter.

"Mary El, do you want to go and help you mom with a salad for us?"

Mary Ellen met her dad's gaze. She understood. He was stepping up. Saying he wanted a word with her boyfriend. She was so thrilled at that, that she didn't even resent being relegated to the kitchen with her mom.

Antonio dropped a kiss on top of her head and smiled as she followed her mom into the kitchen. He knew what was going on, too, and it seemed he was fine with it.

When they reached the kitchen, her mom closed the door behind them and Mary Ellen braced herself. She needn't have worried. Her mom smiled at her with tears in her eyes. "Oh, Mary Ellen. He's lovely!"

Mary Ellen's eyes filled up, too, as she hugged her. "I know, Mom. I'm glad you can see it."

Her mom leaned back and waggled her eyebrows. "I don't think there's a woman on earth who could miss it. You've done so well for yourself."

For a moment, Mary Ellen tensed. She wanted her mom to see beyond his looks and his charm and wealth. She wanted her to know the man and to understand just how well she really had done for herself. She relaxed. She should just be happy that her mom approved. The rest could come—with time— hopefully. "Thank you."

When they were done making salad, they went out to the back yard. She had a feeling that Antonio and her dad would become fast friends. She'd expected it, but it still made her stop in her tracks when she reached the back door and saw them standing there, laughing together in the last of the setting sun. She swallowed around the lump in her throat and swiped at her eyes. Wow. Her world was complete.

Antonio turned and saw her standing there. He held his arm out to her with a smile and she went to him. He closed his arm around her and hugged her into his side in that way that he had. She loved it. It made her feel ... she smiled as she realized just what it made her feel—it made her feel like she belonged. She'd have to tell him that later.

"I was coming to check on you both, but you seem to be getting along."

Her dad laughed. "That's an understatement. We're doing great, aren't we, Antonio?"

"We are. In fact, we were just figuring out when your parents can come and visit us."

Mary Ellen eyed them both warily. She wondered how much he'd said. She hadn't mentioned anything to her parents about them living together—since technically, they weren't yet. She needn't have worried. The two of them were grinning at each other, as if they were in on some secret she knew nothing about. "That'll be nice." She didn't know what else to say.

Her mom had gone back into the kitchen and came out with a tray of glasses and a pitcher of lemonade. She frowned at her husband. "You should pour your beer into a glass."

Apparently, he was ready to assert himself. He just smiled and raised his bottle and said, "No, thanks," before taking a swig.

Antonio came and poured a glass of lemonade and handed it to her mom, before turning to her. "I should have stopped to pick up Margarita mix on the way here."

She laughed. "I'll take a beer." She gave her mom an apologetic smile as he handed her one and she took a drink from the bottle.

To her delight, her mom chuckled and set down her lemonade. "Well, if you can't beat them, then I suppose you just have to join them. Would you pass me one, Bill?"

Mary Ellen buried her smile in Antonio's shoulder as her dad popped the top off a bottle and brought it to her. He wrapped his arm around her shoulders and kissed her cheek. "There you go, Vee. Relax and enjoy yourself."

It made Mary Ellen want to cry happy tears. It was the most intimate moment she'd ever witnessed between the two of them, and it was all thanks to Antonio. She smiled up at him gratefully.

He had that look in his eyes again. She'd wondered, that first night he'd spoken to her at Molly's, what it would be like if he cared for her for real, like a boyfriend. Now she knew. His eyes shone with love and it was all for her. She reached up and planted a kiss on his lips. "Thank you for coming here. I love you."

He nodded and cupped her face between his hands. "And I love you. That's why I'm here." He shot a look at her dad who nodded. Mary Ellen sensed a change in him. His smile was still there, but if anything, he seemed a little tense—nervous? No. Antonio didn't do nervous. Then she understood as he dropped on one knee before her and held up a ring. "I love you, Mary Ellen. You know I do. I want to spend the rest of my life loving you. I want us to have babies and grandbabies and grow old together. I know we haven't been together very long, but I also know the truth of my heart. Please, say you'll be my wife—just as soon as you're ready."

Her hand flew up to cover her mouth. She hadn't expected this. She looked down into his big brown eyes, they shone with hope and with love. He looked uncertain, as if she might say no. She looked at her parents; they were clinging to each other, watching her expectantly. She grinned at Antonio. "Yes! Yes, I want to marry you. I'm ready."

He slid the ring onto her finger and got to his feet. "You're ready?"

She nodded eagerly. There was nothing left to think about. He was it for her. He was the one. There was no point delaying getting started on their future.

Her parents came and hugged them both. She was relieved how happy they both seemed. Her dad raised his glass. "Here's to the two of you. You have my blessing and my best wishes for a long and happy future together."

"And mine." Her mom raised her bottle and took a drink of her beer. "We'll need to start making plans, Mary Ellen."

Mary Ellen nodded. She wasn't sure how she felt about planning a wedding again. This was different; it was Antonio, but still, it wasn't a prospect she relished.

Antonio dropped a kiss on top of her head. It seemed he understood. "How would you feel about not making any plans?"

She looked up at him. "What do you mean?"

"I mean," he looked over at her dad, who nodded encouragingly. "We could get married at our house. Have it catered, have all the arrangements made quickly and easily. You wouldn't have to do a thing if you don't want to. You could just go dress shopping with Chelsea and the girls."

She grinned at him, she knew how impatient he was. "When you say quickly, just how quickly are you thinking?"

He dropped his head and looked up at her from under his eyebrows. "Next weekend?"

"Next weekend?!" She and her mom both spoke at the same time.

"Why not?" asked her dad. "If it's what you both want, why not just do it? I never understood why planning a wedding had to take so long. You end up getting lost in the arrangements and missing out on the fun it's supposed to be." He looked at Mary Ellen. "Don't you want to?"

Mary Ellen looked up at Antonio. He looked so earnest. "We can do it however, whenever you want. I'll wait if that's what you want, but you know me."

She nodded. She did know him, and she knew herself too. Her dad was right. She'd get lost in the planning—like Cam had—and miss out on what it was really about. She cupped Antonio's face between her hands and kissed him. "Let's do it."

Chapter Twenty

Antonio checked himself over in the mirror and smiled. He looked good.

Marcos came to stand beside him and nodded. "She's a lucky girl."

"No. I'm the lucky one."

Marcos nodded. "I believe you are. She's a great girl. I would never have put you with her, but then you always surprise me."

Antonio met his gaze and smiled. "I'm smarter than I make out. When it's time to play, I play. When it's time to work, I work. And when it's time to meet a woman and settle down, I find the best woman there is and make her my wife."

Marcos laughed. "Yes, and you don't waste any time about it. This time last week, you were back at home, helping me sort my mess out. If you'd have told me then that you'd be getting married in a week …" He shook his head. "If you'd told me I'd be back here, in California, I would have laughed in your face."

Antonio gripped his shoulder. "Things don't have to take as long as you expect, you know."

Marcos shook his head. "If you're talking about Molly, it's too soon. I planned to come see her—after I've spent some time getting right with myself. I know she'll be here today, but ..."

He shook his head again. "The timing isn't right."

"Maybe not, but I'm glad you'll get to her."

"Me too."

They both looked up at the sound of a knock on the door. "Come in," called Antonio.

The door opened, and he smiled at the sight of his parents standing there. "We wanted a moment with you."

They came in and his dad closed the door behind them. "We have a wedding gift."

Antonio raised an eyebrow. "Should we wait until later? What about Mary Ellen?"

"It's a gift that will be for both of you once you're married, but we wanted to do this now. With just the four of us."

"Okay." Antonio wasn't sure what they might want to give him, but he smiled. "What is it?"

His dad opened his jacket and took out an envelope. "Read it and see."

Antonio took the envelope and looked at his mom and Marcos. They both smiled eagerly.

He tore it open and read the document inside, then blew out a long breath. "Guys, you can't do this. I mean, thank you, but ..."

He turned to look at Marcos, but his brother just laughed. "Don't worry. I was the one who suggested it."

"But I can't take it. The estate? The winery? It belongs in the family. To all of us, and in the future, to you and me. Then to our children."

Marcos shook his head. "The estate belongs to you already. You've made it what it is. You've earned it. I want you to have it."

Antonio looked at his parents.

His mom smiled. "We won't ever come back here to live. And I hope that when we come to visit you'll allow us to stay."

He chuckled. "As if I wouldn't!"

His dad looked more serious. "You're starting your own family now, Antonio. It's right that you should own the place, be in charge of your own destiny—and your own legacy."

Antonio nodded. He was thrilled and shocked at the same time. "Thank you."

His dad hugged him, and his mom came and kissed his cheek. "You're welcome. We're happy for you. We'll see you out there."

Once they'd gone, Antonio sat down on his bed and looked at his brother. "Are you sure about this?"

Marcos nodded. "I am. Don't give it another thought. It's helping me."

"Helping you? How?"

Marcos came and sat down beside him and met his gaze in the mirror. "I fucked my life up, I did my best to fuck the business up. From here on out I'm making a fresh start, and I want to do it all on my own. I don't want the support of the family—at least, not financially. I want to start from scratch and build something of my own, all by myself. I need to be hungry for something and become a self-made man. Then I might be able to look myself in the eye again."

Antonio slung an arm around his shoulders. "Okay. I get it. You don't want the financial support, but don't forget you have my brotherly support."

Marcos smiled. "I know it, and I have a feeling I'm going to need it." He looked at his watch. "For now, it's me who needs to do the brotherly support and get you out onto the terrace before your bride goes out there."

They both got to their feet and Antonio's eyes welled with tears as they hugged.

~ ~ ~

"Would you quit fidgeting!" Chelsea was standing behind her, pulling up the zipper on her dress.

"I'm not fidgeting! I just can't believe I've gained weight since we bought this! It's only been four days."

Chelsea stood back. "You haven't gained weight! Don't be ridiculous. Look at you! You're beautiful." She turned Mary Ellen around, so she was facing the mirror.

Mary Ellen stared at herself and nodded happily. "I'm not even going to argue. I scrub up okay, don't I?"

Chelsea laughed. "You sure do, and you shop like a demon!"

Mary Ellen laughed. The week since Antonio had proposed had flown by in a blur. When they'd arrived back in Napa, they'd gathered their friends together to share their news and everyone had stepped up to help out. Cameron had insisted that she take the week off. Chelsea had gone dress shopping with her on Tuesday, and in the course of an hour they'd visited two stores and in the second one had found her gown—and it was perfect. "I just got lucky."

"Well, I wouldn't mind some of your luck. When I'm ready to find my dress, you're coming with me to help."

"You know it!"

Chelsea shook her head. "I'm not sure what I know with you and weddings anymore. I thought it would take you a long time to accept what was going on with you and Antonio. I thought you'd get married next year at the earliest. And I did not expect you to throw caution to the wind and arrange a wedding in under a week. You're making Cam and me look bad. We've been pussy-footing around for months!"

Mary Ellen laughed. "What can I say? I'm more surprised at myself than anyone. But it's so right. I mean, it's Antonio. I love him, and that means at least a part of me must love the way he does things. He's all in, full-on, right now, get it done. I know I prefer being organized and having my timelines, but this is right, for us—we're still on a timeline, it's just a much shorter one."

Chelsea grinned. "It's awesome. I couldn't be happier for you—or for him. We should get moving. You've done so well getting everything ready at warp-speed, we don't want to spoil it by getting you to the altar late."

Mary Ellen smiled. "Or even to the terrace."

"Yeah, it's just a figure of speech. I'm glad you're getting married here."

"I am, too. It's perfect. I love this house. It's going to be our home, so it's right that we should begin our married life right here."

"Come on then, let's go do it."

Chelsea went and opened the bedroom door and peeked out.

"What are you doing?" asked Mary Ellen.

"Making sure there's no one out here who shouldn't see your dress yet."

She heard her dad's voice from out in the hallway. "I want to see it, and it's about time we made our way out there."

Chelsea opened the door wide and Mary Ellen's eyes filled with tears at the way her dad looked at her.

"Oh, Mary El, you look beautiful, love."

She went to him and he wrapped her in a hug.

"I'm so proud of you."

She had to swallow hard.

"Take it easy, you two," said Chelsea with a smile. "I'll have to fix her makeup if she starts crying, and we don't have time for that."

Mary Ellen took her dad's arm and they stood at the top of the grand stairway. She smiled at Chelsea. "Don't worry about us. You get your skinny little butt down there and let them know we're coming."

~ ~ ~

Antonio stood shoulder to shoulder with Marcos under the gazebo on the terrace. This was perfect. There were rows of seats facing him with a little aisle down the middle. He smiled out at all the familiar faces. His parents were on the front row on his side, and at his request, Rodney sat with them. Behind them were his friends. Jack and Pete and their wives. Nate and Lily sat with Smoke and Laura. On the other side of the aisle, Mary Ellen's mom sat smiling at him. She was going to make a better mother-in-law than he'd first thought. She just needed to loosen up a little, and he knew he could help with that. Aunt Madeleine and Uncle Cole sat on the front row with her. He loved that. When they understood how the guest list was working out, they'd asked to be on the bride's side. Mary Ellen was as good as family to them. Behind them sat Cam and Piper and Grant and Molly and a handful of Mary Ellen's friends from Hamilton-Groves. He was sure that between them they could have filled a cathedral with friends and acquaintances, but this was right. This day was for the two of them, and they would share it with the people who meant most to them in the world.

Marcos dug him in the ribs and he looked at the doorway leading out from the living room. He sucked in a deep breath as the music struck up, and then let it out with a chuckle as Chelsea appeared. She looked great, but she wasn't the one he was waiting for.

His laughter dried in his throat as Mary Ellen appeared, holding onto her dad's arm. She looked amazing. The dress was perfect. It molded to her figure, showing off her perfect hour-glass. He closed his eyes for a second against the unexpected stirring in his pants. The wedding night would be here soon enough. Right now wasn't the moment to think about that. Right now he wanted to focus on everything else the love he felt for her meant to him. She was everything. She'd made him into a man, a man he was proud of, a man who was going to love her for the rest of her days and who would be proud to call her his wife.

His chest buzzed with happiness as she met his gaze and smiled. How had he ever been scared of her? She was amazing. She was kind and generous. He could see it in the eyes of everyone she passed as she made her way down the aisle to him. Lyle from the office blew her a kiss as she passed him, and Antonio chuckled as she gave him a stern look. That was why he'd been scared—she stood for no bullshit. He didn't need to fear that anymore—because there'd never be any bullshit between the two of them. He'd given her his heart, and with it, he was making her a solemn promise that would do everything within his power to be the man she needed him to be—to be a man they could both be proud of.

It took forever for her to reach him. When she did, she turned and kissed her dad's cheek. He swiped a tear from his eye as he placed her hand in Antonio's. "Take good care of my little girl," he croaked as he stepped back.

Antonio swallowed the lump in his throat and nodded. "I promise. Always."

He lifted Mary Ellen's hand to his lips and kissed it. "Are you ready to do this?"

She nodded. "I'm ready."

"In that case," said the officiant, "let's begin. Friends, family, we are gathered here today ..."

~ ~ ~

Mary Ellen struggled to focus on the words the officiant was saying. All she could do was stare into Antonio's eyes. He smiled as he held her gaze, and they each spoke their vows. The whole thing was over so quickly. Antonio slid the ring onto her finger, she slid one onto his and then ...

"I now pronounce you man and wife. You may now ..."

Antonio hadn't waited for permission. He'd already slid his arms around her waist and his lips came down on hers. His kiss made her forget where they were, forget that all their friends and family were watching. All she knew was the feel of his arms around her, the feel of their lips crushed against each other, and the overflowing of all the love in her heart for this beautiful man who was now her husband.

When they came up for air, they were met with a cheer from their friends and family. She grinned at them all as she walked back down the little aisle on Antonio's arm. The way they'd rehearsed it was that they would go back into the house and meet the officiant in Antonio's office where they'd sign all the paperwork that made their marriage legal. However, Antonio was deviating from the plan. Instead of taking her back into the house, he was making his way across the terrace toward the side yard. She gave him a puzzled look. "Did you forget about the paperwork?"

He grinned. "No. I just want to show you something first. Trust me?"

She nodded happily. "I do."

When they rounded the corner of the house her eyes filled with tears. This area was a formal garden, with flower beds and grassed areas around a central square. In the middle of the square stood a freshly planted magnolia. She covered her mouth as the tears rolled down her face.

He cupped her cheek, looking worried. "You don't like it?"

"I love it. It's so sweet of you."

He hugged her into his side. "I'm many things, Mary Ellen, but I'm not sweet. I pay attention, like I told you. You said your grandma had a magnolia tree. I wanted you to have one here, so that you can have some sense of your history in our home. I want you to feel like you belong here."

She planted a kiss on his lips. "Thank you. Remember when you told me I should try to feel like I belong? Well, now I don't need to try. I feel it. I do belong, right here, with you, and the tree will always remind me of that."

And it was true. They might seem like an unlikely match in some respects, but they complemented each other, and she knew she'd found the place she belonged in life—and the man she belonged with;

A Note from SJ

I hope you enjoyed spending time with the Hamiltons. Please let your friends know about the books if you feel they would enjoy them as well. It would be wonderful if you would leave me a review; I'd very much appreciate it.

There are so many more stories still to tell. The next book I'm working on is TJ's story which will be out soon in the Davenports' series. After that, we'll go back to Napa for Marcos and Molly's story. After that, I'll get to the third Davenport brother, Reid, just as fast as my little fingers can type. Plus, there are more stories set at the Lake; the pilots want a Summer Lake Flyers series. And there are a bunch of cowboys who are all getting impatient for me to return to Montana. My plan, at the moment, is to finish with the Davenports and Hamiltons and then get to the next three series—Summer Lake Flyers, the new cowboys, who haven't told me what their series is called yet, and the country singers in Nashville, beginning with Autumn and Matt. The older couples are growing impatient, and I've still yet to figure out whether they'll end up as a series or as novellas when they get too impatient to wait any longer. The short version is that there are still a lot of stories to come.

In the meantime, be sure to check out my Remington Ranch series, if you haven't already. You can get started with book one, Mason, which you can download in ebook form FREE from all the major online retailers but they are all available in paperback if you prefer.

If you'd like to keep in touch, there are a few options to keep up with me and my imaginary friends:

The best way is to Join up on the website for my Newsletter. Don't worry I won't bombard you! I'll let you know about upcoming releases, share a sneak peek or two and keep you in the loop for a couple of fun giveaways I have coming up :0)

You can join my readers group to chat about the books on Facebook or just browse and like my Facebook Page.

I occasionally attempt to say something in 140 characters or less(!) on Twitter

And I'm always in the process of updating my website at

www.sjmccoy.com

with new book updates and even some videos. Plus, you'll find the latest news on new releases and giveaways in my blog.

I love to hear from readers, so feel free to email me at AuthorSJMcCoy@gmail.com.. I'm better at that! :0)

I hope our paths will cross again soon. Until then, take care, and thanks for your support—you are the reason I write!

Love

SJ

PS Project Semicolon

You may have noticed that the final sentence of the story closed with a semi-colon. It isn't a typo. Project Semi Colon is a non-profit movement dedicated to presenting hope and love to those who are struggling with depression, suicide, addiction and self-injury. Project Semicolon exists to encourage, love and inspire. It's a movement I support with all my heart.

"A semicolon represents a sentence the author could have ended, but chose not to. The sentence is your life and the author is you."

- Project Semicolon

This author started writing after her son was killed in a car crash. At the time I wanted my own story to be over, instead I chose to honour a promise to my son to write my 'silly stories' someday. I chose to escape into my fictional world. I know for many who struggle with depression, suicide can appear to be the only escape. The semicolon has become a symbol of support, and hopefully a reminder – Your story isn't over yet

Also by SJ McCoy

The Davenports
Oscar
Coming next
TJ

The Hamiltons
Cameron and Piper in Red wine and Roses
Chelsea and Grant in Champagne and Daisies
Mary Ellen and Antonio in Marsala and Magnolias
Coming Next
Marcos and Molly in Prosecco and Peonies

Summer Lake Series
Love Like You've Never Been Hurt (FREE in ebook form)
Work Like You Don't Need the Money
Dance Like Nobody's Watching
Fly Like You've Never Been Grounded
Laugh Like You've Never Cried
Sing Like Nobody's Listening
Smile Like You Mean It
The Wedding Dance
Chasing Tomorrow
Dream Like Nothing's Impossible
Ride Like You've Never Fallen
Live Like There's No Tomorrow
The Wedding Flight

Remington Ranch Series

Mason (FREE in ebook form) and also available as Audio

Shane

Carter
Beau
Four Weddings and a Vendetta

A Chance and a Hope

Chance is a guy with a whole lot of story to tell. He's part of the fabric of both Summer Lake and Remington Ranch. He needed three whole books to tell his own story.

Chance Encounter

Finding Hope

Give Hope a Chance

About the Author

I'm SJ, a coffee addict, lover of chocolate and drinker of good red wines. I'm a lost soul and a hopeless romantic. Reading and writing are necessary parts of who I am. Though perhaps not as necessary as coffee! I can drink coffee without writing, but I can't write without coffee.

I grew up loving romance novels, my first boyfriends were book boyfriends, but life intervened, as it tends to do, and I wandered down the paths of non-fiction for many years. My life changed completely a few years ago and I returned to Romance to find my escape.

I write 'Sweet n Steamy' stories because to me there is enough angst and darkness in real life. My favorite romances are happy escapes with a focus on fun, friendships and happily-ever-afters, just like the ones I write.

These days I live in beautiful Montana, the last best place. If I'm not reading or writing, you'll find me just down the road in the park - Yellowstone. I have deer, eagles and the occasional bear for company, and I like it that way :0)